FEE FI FO FUM

Kevin Sweeney

Black Rainbows Press

For the Godless tribe
My apologies if you didn't die; it was my dearest
wish to kill you all!

"Whatever the fable of Bevis of Southampton, and the *giant in the woods thereabouts* may be derived from, I found the people of Southampton mighty willing to have these things pass for true."

Daniel Defoe

ONCE UPON a time, down in the dark, the lids of strange eyes twitched after centuries of stillness.

Vibrations upon the ground above. Vibrations which were far more regular then the occasional footfall of some human passing unknowing over the resting place. Vibrations which spoke of intense activity.

The clearing of ground.

The breaking of earth.

Digging.

Down in the dark strange eyes opened.

And a stomach began to growl.

*****

The bolt cutters clipped through the last chain link of the fence and then were thrown aside. They'd been nicked just for this one job, so who gave a fuck.

"Cunt Face says, open says me," said Ray Webster.

Saliem almost corrected him, but kept his tongue. *It's open SESAME you prick!*

Dean and Saliem peeled the fence back to let Ray wheel the bike through.

Then they picked up the vodka and followed him in.

The site was only dimly lit by the street lights on the three roads that bounded it, but it was enough to show the mounds of earth that had been piled up, and the deep troughs between them.

You would think it had been made for fucking around on a nicked bike.

The triangle of land was formed by the end of Thomas Lewis Way splitting in two, with the other edge formed by Bevois Hill. There had been a row of Georgian town houses on the Bevois Hill edge, but the rest of it had just been ancient, scrubby trees; where Thomas Lewis Way split before venturing down into the Valley itself with its bars and takeaway shops on the left, there had been erected a giant sculpture that the locals called the Cheese Grater. The houses had been bought with a compulsory purchase order, and the whole site was going to be converted into flats for the city's ever growing population of students. The sculpture, which was supposed to be a sword commemorating the mythical knight Sir Bevis of Hamtun that the valley was named after, was all that was left.

Hoardings had gone up on all sides, except for the fencing which was a temporary night-time barrier pulled across where site traffic entered.

The hoardings meant that even though the site stood at the top end of where the city's students did their drinking -which had made it attractive to the development company- it was nicely secluded, which was just what Ray and his boys wanted.

The filth had been coming down hard lately back on their own estate, part of the semi-annual half-hearted attempt to deal with anti-social behaviour, so for the time being Ray had deemed it best to stay off the main roads. A lot of his crew had had their collars felt, and another turn in front of a Judge would see good old Cunt Face himself entering the juvenile correction facilities of Her Majesty's Pleasure.

The bike nicking went on, of course, but they needed a more discreet place to rag the fuck out of them.

Dean's brother had picked up a bit of labouring work on the site, and had told Dean that the development company were too fucking cheap to hire security just yet, so, you know...

Dean's brother had also bought them the vodka. Working cash in hand, he'd felt flush.

These facts, and having to stay off the estate for a bit until the fucking filth fucked off, had put Ray in a bit of a bad mood.

They were *his* boys now, Cunt Face's crew. Dean's brother had had his time as king of the estate, but now it was turn to rule, to make his legend. He was the one who decided what they got up to at night, and since when did they ever pay for their drink? It wasn't just a matter of principle to rip off the Paki shops around their estate, it was a logical thing as well; didn't make sense, did it, to nick some prick's moped which was worth a few hundred, but then go and pay for a bottle of voddy?

But he couldn't kick up too much of a stink, because using the building site as their own private motor-cross course was actual a pretty good fucking idea.

That, and Dean's brother was still a hard cunt, even if he was ancient now. Twenty-two? Fuck off granddad.

Ray surveyed the site.

The fencing was high all along the edges where the roads were, but the scrubby bit of brush behind it that separated it from the industrial estate only had a token bit of chain link thrown up. Easy work with the bolt clippers nicked from his neighbours shed.

As Dean's brother put it, they'd only finished clearing away a lot of the rotten old trees and undergrowth a few days before, scraping everything back to dirt ready to bring in heavy plant next week. When there were diggers and bulldozers actually being used here and stored overnight, security would be brought in, but for now there was just a pre-fabricated office cabin and a portable toilet to indicate what the place was for.

That and mounds of dirt to ramp up.

Satisfied, Ray turned to his boys and snapped his fingers.

"Cunt Face wants his voddy," he said.

Dean passed him the bottle.

Ray had a long pull.

"Jesus Fuck," he said. "Fuck, Deany boy, Kev didn't push the fucking boat out did he? The fuck is this shit, it's like fucking paint stripper."

In the half-light, Dean dared to look annoyed.

"He didn't have to..." he said, before Ray cut him off.

"Didn't have to, shouldn't have fucking bothered more like. Cunt Face wants a smoke, yeah?"

Saliem produced one of the joints he'd rolled at home.

Ray snatched it, and tucked it in the good corner of his mouth.

There was a pause. A late night taxi passed by on the far side road. The scent of kebab drifted over from the Valley.

"It's not going to fucking light itself," said Ray.

"Yeah, sorry," said Saliem, rummaging out a Clipper lighter and sparking up. He was still on *probation*, and was well aware that he wasn't out of the territory of having his head kicked in just yet. The fact that his cousin was part of a county lines operation out of London giving him access to a steady supply of good shit was the only reason the likes of Ray "Cunt Face" Webster and his crew hadn't already given him a good toeing.

Ray filled his lungs, and then released two streams of gorgeous smelling smoke.

"Fuuuucckk," he moaned. "You know Sally, for a filthy Muzzy, you roll a half-decent bifta, you're mate Cunt Face here is already half-cunted."

"Thanks," said Saliem. He'd learned to be brief with Ray, and only speak when spoken to.

And you sure as shit didn't question why he talked about himself in the third-person.

As if the thick bastard even knew what third-person was, Saliem thought.

Taking another drag on the good side of his mouth, Ray held it in his lungs and passed the joint to Dean.

A small wisp curled out of the harelip that split the left hand side of his philtrum right up to the nostril.

Saliem looked away. Even though Ray Webster had taken on the nickname he had been abused with all through school, making it his own in defiance, he was still sensitive about the source. *Cunt-face* Anyone who he thought was looking straight at his harelip was liable to end up with three inches of Stanley blade waved in their face with an offer to give them a matching gash of their own, turning them into yet another "cunt face".

Saliem had asked Dean a few weeks before whether Ray had actually done it to anyone, y'know, cut them.

Dean had said, yeah, Star.

Ray's own sister.

Slit her upper lip straight up the middle.

Dean blew a smoke ring and passed the joint to Saliem.

Ray released a stream of smoke straight upwards, like a mushroom cloud.

"*Fuuuuccccckkkk*," he croaked, and coughed. "Fuck. Here Sally, you said your cousin can get plenty of this shit, yeah?"

"Yeah," said Saliem.

"Hmm. Cunt Face might want a little word in your ear about something later."

Saliem kept his face blank, but inside he grinned.

Ray nodded, took a pull on the vodka bottle and passed it to Dean. Then he swung his leg over the bike they had stolen earlier and settled himself into the seat.

"Vroom vroom," he said, and kicked it into life.

It was only a rat bike, and the sound of its engine starting up was not a deep throated roar, but more like the sound of an angry wasp caught in an empty biscuit tin. Still, who gave a fuck, they were just going to rag the fuck out of it anyway.

Ray gripped the joint between his teeth and pulled away into the dimly lit dunes of turned earth. The bikes wheels sent loose stones and dry dirt spraying out behind him as he revved it up too hard and too fast, wobbling slightly, until he gained momentum and balance.

For quarter of an hour Dean and Saliem watched Ray tear up and down the length of the site, from time to time gunning the engine to take on one of the mounds of dirt, each time ramping into the air and crashing down so hard it seemed the poor little scooter would have to break... and yet it didn't.

Eventually he pulled up alongside them again and pulled the stub of the joint from his mouth.

"You know what, Sally" he said, voice croaking. "Cunt Face normally wouldn't have nothing to do with a Muzzy, but this shit is..."

Saliem had been playing the racist dickhead along. He knew he couldn't start selling around the estate or in their school without getting approval from Ray. And in those few words ("You know what...") he had heard the start of that approval.

But then it was interrupted.

"Oi, who are you? You shouldn't be here, clear off!"

As one, the three boys turned.

In the gloom it was hard to see, but the voice belonged to an old man, and the tiny silhouette that was advancing towards them didn't exactly trigger a flight response in them.

Dean looked to Ray.

Ray was grinning.

Saliem felt a knot of dread in his guts, and frustration. He'd been so close to getting Ray's approval, and now there was this...

The old man stopped in front of them. In the dim light and shadows it was hard to make him out, but he was wearing glasses and a shapeless old coat and he smelled strongly of peppermints and cigarettes.

"I don't know who you are, but I know you shouldn't be hanging around here!" the old man said. "Piss off before I call the coppers!"

"Now, now, granddad," said Ray pleasantly. "We're just minding our own fucking business, not doing nothing to nobody, so why don't you fuck off before you get hurt, yeah? It's really not safe for you here."

The old man wasn't intimidated.

"This isn't a safe place for anybody!" he shouted. "We've been keeping watch for centuries! Do you have any idea what that's like, what kind of a fucking burden it is? I told those cunts at the council not to sell, but did they listen? This ground was never supposed to be disturbed, never!"

Saliem alone amongst the three boys picked up the underlying terror in the man's voice. The knot in his guts tightened.

Ray was willing to play along for a moment or so.

"Granddad, granddad, oh poor old granddad, whatever has got your fucking knickers in a knot?" he chided.

Dean sniggered.

"This was where we put him down!" said the silhouette of a man. "They didn't know why they put the sword up here, not in their heads they didn't, but in their hearts they did, because the blood remembers! The blood remembers!"

"The blood remembers what?" asked Ray.

"Blood!" cried the old man. "Blood remembers blood! The ground is soaked in it! It's sodden with it! Here, where he finally fell and we piled all that bloody earth on top of him until he couldn't get up again... and now they're scraping it off! For flats! For fucking flats! What was the point, eh? Answer me that! What was the fucking point of my family guarding this place for so many fucking years..."

The old man ranted on.

Ray was bored.

Saliem felt the air grow taut.

"Flats! Fucking flats! Say they're going up quick, they do, but not quick enough!" the shadowy figure that smelled of peppermints and tobacco was pulling at its face and moaning. "Quick, quick, pour the concrete before he stirs! Nice long nap he's had, chance to heal up, a thousand years..."

In his delirium and in the gloom he didn't see the threat until Ray was on him, driving a powerful young fist into the yammering mouth.

The older man fell back with a squawk, arms turning windmills as his heels betrayed him on the unsteady ground. A hail of blood sprayed the dirt. He sprawled out on his back, and then Ray was on him, kicking him once, twice, three times, each kick earning another new sound of pain and outrage from his victim.

After the first three blows, he stopped and looked at his boys.

His eyes were almost entirely empty, glistening frogspawn in the dim light.

He never spoke an order, but gave them two heartbeats to make a crucial decision.

Dean was faster than Saliem, but only by a moment in which Saliem felt the balance of his soul tip a little further into the shade.

Though planning a lucrative career in dealing, he still thought of himself as better than these mindless thugs he believed he was manipulating.

And yet...

His first kick was an unlucky shot. He heard, and felt, a rib break.

Dean laughed like a hyena and stomped on the man's belly.

The old man vomited, his dinner blowing over his lips and onto his face and the air suddenly smelled of tinned chicken curry.

"You nasty old fucker," growled Ray.

Then it became a frenzy, the three young men, barely more than boys, all laying the boot in like some kind of group animal with six legs, adrenaline driving their glorious hate.

Even Saliem lost that innate sense that he was different, that he was better, as he got to join in as an *equal*. Later he might have reflected on how violence could be a bonding experience as much as familial or cultural ties.

But for Saliem and Dean and Ray there was no later.

Blood was spilled upon the disturbed earth of centuries, and deep in the darkness beneath them a strange mouth opened.

At some point, the old man had stopped twitching, had stopped groaning or weakly crying out as his attackers kicked and punched him.

His skull was fractured. His ribs were snapped. His brain was bleeding.

Twin drools of blood were leaking from the corners of his mouth, rolling down his cheeks to patter onto the dirt he was lying face-up upon, soaking into the ground… which was stirring.

His attackers didn't notice.

As one, as if some unspoken command compelled them, they finally stopped laying into their victim.

Ray was grinning, panting.

Dean just looked blank.

And Saliem suddenly found himself calculating how many years inside they were all going to get for killing a defenceless old man.

Time to start getting your story straight.

They stood in a loose triangle around the prone body of the man they had beaten and then something broke through the surface of the churned earth a dozen yards feet behind Cunt Face. Dean saw it first, as he was facing that direction.

It was a hand.

A hand the size of a door.

It gripped the earth, scoring long furrows as fingers the size of arms dug in to secure its grip and then tensed, ready to drag more of itself upwards.

Ray was still grinning, staring down at their work… but the strange sound Saliem made as he spotted what Dean was looking at made their leader look at them.

Dean could never have been as eloquent as his expression.

Saliem moaned, an animal sound of despair as his bladder let go.

Ray followed their line of sight, and turned around just as the thing's head broke through the ground, earth tumbling away in clods.

The worst thing, the most awful thing, was that even though its features were not human, its expression was unmistakable.

Glee.

Ray Webster's last coherent thought was not one of insight and wit.

What the fuck…?

Awe kept them rooted in place as the thing hauled itself out of the grave of centuries.

It was something like a foetus, and something like an elephant rearing up on hind legs, though without trunk or tusks or ears. The great nodding head was the size of a small car, with the body only a little larger, short but thick limbs and enormous hands. A giant aborted baby, grey and wrinkled skin with dozens of ancient scars criss-crossing it.

Even hunched over as it was by carrying its vast head, if the boys had stood on each other's shoulders like acrobats they would barely have been able to look it in the eyes.

The boulder of its head was hairless and almost without features.

Just eyes and a mouth.

The last thought that any of the boys would have would belong to Saliem after his brain fully took in what it was looking at, and tried to frame some context for something so utterly wrong.

Two eyes, set in the middle of the expanse of grey and wrinkled flesh, so close set they could have been taken for nostrils if blood coloured orbs the size of skulls hadn't been sat deep in the sockets.

And the mouth... a wide curve, a lipless crescent that ran from where one ear should have been to where the other was not, a huge idiot smile like someone had carved into the grey flesh with a machete, their hand shaking as they cut.

And here came that final thought, as Saliem's mind sought a reference for such a bizarre face that loomed over them like the moon slowly descending.

He remembered his mum and dad taking him and his brothers to a pantomime. His parents had come from Pakistan, but had determined to raise their sons as British as they could, and that meant soaking them in every aspect of the culture. So, come Christmas time they had a visit from Father Christmas, and they ate bland roast turkey and watched the Queen's speech and they had gone to see the pantomime at the Mayflower theatre.

They'd only gone the once. As eager to embrace their new home as they were, Saliem's parents were still conservative Muslims. The cross-dressing and smutty jokes hadn't sat well with them.

Saliem remembered *Jack & the Beanstalk.*

That was the memory, and this was his last rational thought;

Fee-fi-fo-fum!

Then the mouth opened and *snapped* and Ray Webster's entire body right down to the drawstring of his tracksuit bottoms was engulfed.

Through muscle and bones and organs teeth the size of broken dinner plates slid as easily as razors through eyelids.

The foetal giant lifted its mouthful and tilted its head back, swallowing in a series of awkward jerks.

Ray Webster's legs stayed standing, a stub of spinal column sticking out of the back of his tracksuit bottoms as loops of severed intestines stirred like worms chopped in half by a spade.

Dean and Saliem were urban animals, their instincts honed to different threats than those of their far distant ancestors who knew the terror of not being at the top of the food chain. As such, they did not take the opportunity available in those few precious seconds where they might, just might, have been able to save themselves by fleeing from the feeding ground.

Cunt Face's legs toppled. They hit the ground and kicked twice, that stub of spinal column sending its last confused electrical impulses.

Ascupart was lost in the sensation of genetic material tumbling into himself, a DNA source that was screaming as it slithered in a slew of its own blood and guts down his throat. Alive, still alive, as it fell into his stomach; he could feel tiny hands clawing at the lining of his belly as the material tried to save itself.

But the sound of feet drumming the earth changed the focus of his attention.

The other little ones were still there, looking up at him.

He spotted the twitching legs.

And nearby, frozen to the spot, more little ones.

Dark happiness bloomed within him like a poisonous night-flower as he reached for the other material that still hadn't the sense to run screaming before it was too late.

Vast hands wrapped around them both, one bunched in each fist; he gripped slowly, felt the interesting crunching of pelvis bones and ribs crushing between his powerful fingers.

He held them up to his eyes, to peer more closely.

Ah. He sensed the darker skinned one had far great neural activity than the other. Good.

He could watch.

Ascupart, unlike most predators, preferred his food flavoured with adrenaline.

His mouth opened, just a sliver, just enough to gently tweeze the skull of the dimmer mind between his teeth.

He winked at the dark skinned DNA source, and bit the top off Dean's skull as a prelude to delicately tonguing the brain free, the twin tendrils of his split tongue like chopsticks tweezing and squeezing and plucking it out.

The tiny ball of electrified fat slid down into the hot darkness where Ray Webster was dying in absolute horror, telling himself over and over that this was a nightmare and he was going to wake up, wake up, wake up….

Ascupart dropped the rest of that food upon the dirt, and peered closely at… *Sal-eem?* Yes! He could feel the texture of its consciousness, and that was what it called itself.

The genetic material known as human was so fond of assigning meaningless sounds to itself and its environment, as if it could bind the chaos of creation with grunts and clicks.

SALIEM, this one thought of itself.

And there was something else… more nonsense.

Fee... fi... fo... fum...

It blinked at him.

"Ars-koo-part?" it wheezed, a question.

Yes, that's what the genetic material had called him long before. He actually enjoyed having the strange sounds assigned to him, and found perverse pleasure in having his prey know the name of what was eating them.

This one felt his consciousness being abraded, could glean those syllables from the giant's mind as easily as his own had been taken, and so name its death.

Purest delight.

Fee... fi... fo... fum...

Why did the SALIEM keep thinking those sounds?

FEE FI FO FUM I SMELL THE BLOOD OF AN ENGLISHMAN!

Nonsense.

Ascupart lifted the SALIEM and nipped its belly open.

He sensed the pain flash in the material's head, the agony of being gutted.

Ascupart wormed the tip of its tongue into the gaping wound and lapped up intestines, liver, kidneys; deeper, he licked at the dangling lungs and heart, the flavour almost as enjoyable as the vicarious sensation of feeling the human's horror as it realised exactly what was happening to it.

He held it at arm's length.

The eyes were wide and staring at eternity, sanity blasted.

The fun was over.

He pinched the head between thumb and fore finger, and squeezed until the skull buckled, brains bursting from the eye sockets like pus from burst pimples.

A forked tongue the size of a coffin lid lapped the muck from the little one's cheeks as Ascupart took stock.

There was another light nearby, another gently glowing bundle of neurons sparking across synapses… on the ground.

Genetic material that was asleep… no, not sleeping, but not thinking either. Dying.

No joy to be had from that one.

But… all around him, muffled by stone and metal, many, many more minds of little ones glowed. Much more DNA to be acquired, and much, much more joy to be had.

Unbidden, the meaningless syllables which constituted the SALIEM's last thought echoed in the giant's head

FEE FI FO FUM.

He grinned.

Ecstatic to be loose in the world once more, Ascupart held his arms wide apart for support and stumbled like a newborn from the burial ground.

*****

Jack Moores was staring out the window of his bedroom with the taste of his dad's semen still in his mouth, the man's parting words to him still fresh in his ears.

Freshly spoken, not freshly minted; they were the same words every time this happened.

"You look so much like your mum."

An excuse. A reason. An accusation.

A mantra.

Or possibly a punchline, thought Jack. He wasn't sure; like most forms of narrative, jokes baffled him. Perhaps, perhaps, his father forcing him to provide oral sex was some sort of joke.

It made as much sense as any other he'd heard.

Downstairs, the front door closed as PC Moores left for his shift.

Jack watched his father leave their terraced house and jog between the closely parked cars to the patrol vehicle idling in the road. He was already dressed for his shift in his uniform, stab vest, and hi-vis jacket; he and his partner took weekly turns actually heading into the station to clock in and collect a police car for their night shift, so that the other could just wait to get picked up at their front door.

Plenty of time for a blowjob before work.

The car pulled away, heading for an easy evening. It was Tuesday, not a big drinking night, and only days from the Easter break, so even the city's student population who would have made up the bulk of those in the pubs and bars was greatly reduced as many headed home for the long weekend.

It was dark. Jack could see the ghost of his reflection in the glass before him, and so in turn the ghost of his mother.

"You look so much like your mum."

On the bedside dresser behind him, his phone vibrated, buzzing like a huge wasp as its body rattled rapidly on the wooden surface.

It was Astra.

THE FILTH FUKK OFF YET???

Jack winced; he hated the way she spelled the swear word. And Astra knew that, she knew it bothered him. And the unnecessary extra questions marks.

He replied.

MY FATHER HAS LEFT FOR WORK, IF THAT IS WHAT YOU MEAN.

He waited.
She replied.

FUKKIN TWAT!!!

He gritted his teeth, irritated. She was calling him a twat because he used correct syntax and punctuation, and made whole sentences.

Jack hurried from his room and downstairs, into the kitchen and then out the back door to the stub of a rear garden. He reached the back gate that opened into the alley behind the houses and with his usual rush of fear at the chaos he was letting into his life, he opened it for the young lady who called herself his girlfriend.

Astra was tucking her phone into the mutilated *My Little Pony* lunchbox she used as a handbag, the cartoon ponies depicted having had their eyes scratched out and crude word balloons added declaring things like '*Hail S8-10!!!*' and '*GoD hAs AbANDoneD uS.*'

"About fucking time!"

She pushed passed him, heading for the house, glancing back impatiently as she went.

"The fuck are you waiting for? I told my mates we're meeting them at ten."

Astra was at the back door before she realised he hadn't moved.

"What are you playing at Jack?" she asked.

He almost told her.

But then he didn't.

He didn't know if it was the right time, or what the right words were. He didn't even know what he was supposed to be feeling; he'd never got the script.

Astra stared at him, one hand on her hip. She had purple hair on the side of her head that wasn't shaved clean, and three cobalt rings through her upper lip, and even though she was considerably overweight she wore the clothes of a loli goth.

They had known each other in secondary school, but only by sight, and had ended up going to the same college because half of their year group went to the same place. Six months after starting, Astra had sought him out and told him that from that point on, they were an item.

Jack accepted this as he accepted everything in his life...because he had never got the script, and seeing as though everyone else had already learned their lines, he tried to pretend he knew them too.

"Nothing," he said. "I'm not playing at anything."

She rolled her eyes.

"Then get in here and nosh me."

Jack followed his girlfriend into his house, to eat her out before she told him what they were doing that evening.

*****

"I am so, so, so... cunted."

In the beer garden of The Hobbit there was a general noise of agreement in response to this statement, various sounds which were almost words; it was Jesus John who had spoken the sentiment aloud, but the other five who had also partaken of the joint wanted it to be known that they too were so, so, so... cunted.

"That's some good shit," croaked Polly.

This didn't add much to the conversation, but was also universally agreed upon with incoherent vocalisations.

"You said your cousin got this?" Gasman Tim asked Gideon.

Gideon could only nod. He pushed his dreads back and closed his eyes and drifted on the waves of the ocean in his own head. Talking was beyond him.

"I do think I'll be placing a regular order," said Gasman Tim, still in his British Gas uniform, straight from work and sticking out like a sore thumb as the only member of the crew who had regular full-time employment. The neon pink and green bi-hawk he sported was the only real clue he belonged to this clan. "You going to give me his number?"

"Whose number?" asked Zena, trying to shuffle the cards. The steampunk style goggles resting on her forehead gave her an insect appearance, and when she cocked her head asking a question the effect was distinctly praying mantis-like.

"I was talking to Gid."

"Oh. Right. Yeah." She put the deck down. "Who wanted the reading?"

It being a Tuesday night in early April just before Easter, they had the beer garden to themselves, and seeing as though they were amongst the few paying customers across the threshold of the legendary pub that day, the bar staff were turning an even blinder eye than usual to the fact that they were smoking gear in the rear.

The Hobbit stood at the top end of Bevois Valley and was usually the starting point for pub crawls along the length of Bevois Valley Road. It was also popular as a place for the alternative crowd, the various tribes of metal heads, hippies, crusties, punks, goths, and numerous other sub-cultures, a watering hole where the more unlikely urban fauna would congregate.

Though split across three levels with music most nights, the beer garden was the heart of the pub. Because The Hobbit was at the top of a hill, the beer garden was a series of stepped terraces like the side of a ziggurat, with tables on each level, irregularly lit by mock Victorian streetlamps, Chinese lanterns, and strings of fairy lights. It was halfway down that the six sat passing around a funny cigarette of semi-lethal strength, each drawing deep lungfuls of the pungent smoke and releasing them skywards towards the light pollution.

Jesus John, Polly, Gasman Tim, Stokes, Zena, and Gideon were a good cross-section of the pub's clientele.

On the table were half filled glasses, cigarette lighters, rolling tins, mobile phones, Stoke's sketch book in which he had just given up trying to design a tattoo for Polly after the mercurial motherfucker kept changing his mind, and a deck of Aleister Crowley's "Thoth" tarot cards.

"Me," said Jesus John. The nickname was ironic, seeing as though he was a death metal bassist; the Messiah in corpse paint.

"Me?" asked Polly. He pulled his fake fur coat closer around his shoulders, wishing he'd worn something heavier than the tie-dye summer dress he'd chosen for that evening; he'd thought that the fake mink and the Ugg boots would be enough to keep the chill off, but so far it was just the weed doing that. Polly got all his clothes from second-hand shops, and hated to be seen in the same outfit twice. "Me? Cold I am, my lovely, *awfully* cold!"

Jesus John sat up straighter, passed the joint to Stokes who took it with both hands, fingers pinching around the end like it was a tiny flute he was going to play.

"Me," repeated Jesus John. "I'm the one. The reading. Oh fuck me!" He shook his head slowly. "Zena, you were doing me a reading."

Zena looked puzzled.

"Is Azzie here yet?" she asked. "Stokes?"

"She should be," said Stokes. He was staring at the backs of his hands; one had a broken toothed grin tattooed across it, and the other had pouting red lips sewn shut with barb wire. The idea was to cup your mouth with either palm and create an instant statement, but right now, stoned out of his box, the apprentice tattoo artist was staring at them and waiting for them to speak. "With what's his face."

"Oh yeah. Him. Astra and what's his face."

"Wasn't she talking about going to that thing later on?"

"What thing?"

"The book thing, in West Quay. The midnight thing... Gid, you know the book thing right? You said you're mum was going to protest at it..."

"Zena!"

"*What?*"

Jesus John had picked up the tarot cards. He wagged them at her.

"You said you were going to do a reading for me."

"I did?"

Gideon giggled.

He'd just opened his eyes after floating on his private ocean for a hundred years and he had seen something.

What he had seen wasn't funny.

He giggled when he was nervous, or high. And right now he was both.

He pointed at what had made him giggle, but no-one was paying attention.

Gasman Tim drained his pint of Doombar and went to stand up to go inside to the bar, but found that wasn't going to happen for the next twenty minutes at least as his legs had all the strength of overcooked noodles.

"Oh fuck me Gid, you've got to give me your cousin's moby, this shit is... it's fucking shit! I am so fucked up!"

Gideon giggled again.

It was still looking at him.

He'd tried closing his eyes again, but when he'd opened them *it* was still there, looking over the wall at him.

Zena had taken the cards from Jesus John and performed an awkward shuffle before placing them down in the middle of the table.

"Alright, cut the deck, and then flip over the top card, and that will be, uhh, something."

"Some *thing*," emphasised Polly, gripping his fake fur coat tightly around his thin shoulders. "Where's the joint gone? Stokes? Stokes, you twat, you're bogarting!"

Actually, he'd been trying to get the tattooed cartoon mouths on the backs of his hands to take a drag.

"Fucking drama queen," said Stokes.

"Drama *king*," said Polly, who turned all gender norms on their head as a matter of principle.

Jesus John cut the deck. He turned over the top card.

DEATH. A stylized black skeleton wearing a strange crown and wielding a scythe.

"The Universe is Change," intoned Zena, reciting from memory somehow, despite the good gear. "Every Change is the effect of an Act of Love; all Acts of Love contain Pure Joy. Die daily."

Before Jesus John could ask what the fuck that was supposed to mean, the end of their lives began.

Gideon sobbed, and then Ascupart blundered over the wall at the rear of the beer garden from where he had been watching the food.

When his full weight hit the ground it sent a shockwave right up the stepped slope of the beer garden, causing the empty glasses on the table to rattle. Beneath feet with irregular numbers of fist-sized toes, the paving slabs shattered.

The giant had crouched as it hit the ground, and now slowly straightened up, even as the eyes of the five smoking pub patrons turned in his direction.

He looked up at them, and they looked down at him.

His mind scraped against theirs.

FEE FI FO FUM.

They were young. If the adage about life passing before your eyes at the end were true, they each would have had just enough time.

Ascupart tottered forward, arms outstretched like a baby learning to walk. He fell at the first step, an avalanche of wrinkled grey flesh, crushing a wooden table under his bulk, and then on all fours began to crawl up towards the food.

Zena whimpered.

Gideon giggled.

Jesus John said, "Oh shit."

Polly and Stokes pissed themselves.

Gasman Tim, who had hi-jacked the joint from Polly in the seconds after the monster had crashed into the garden, took a long drag, and with an amazing level of detached calm, thought; *If I'd been able to get up to go the bar, I wouldn't be here right now. I'd have been a survivor.*

They watched almost like a single mind as the thing eagerly crawled towards them, taking the steps three at a time, crashing aside tables as if they were nothing, for all the world like a colossal baby eager to get to the toys it wished to play with.

Zena tried to stand and toppled over backwards onto her arse.

Within moments, the monster was looming over their table, its giant head blotting the light-polluted sky even though it was still on all fours.

Polly raised his hands.

He was closest.

"No, don't-"

Ascupart grabbed. His door sized hand wrapped around Polly's entire upper body and snapped shut, crushing; blood and muscle and skin exploded from between fingers the size of a man's arms.

Zena scuttled backwards under the table behind theirs, unable to look away as the thing clapped its hand to its enormous mouth, cramming Polly's crushed body in head first like a greedy child stuffing its face... and began to chew with its mouth open, fake fur and organs and bones being ground between huge teeth, go-go booted legs waggling in the air, being drawn in slowly like tree branches are drawn down the chute of a wood chipper.

Stokes stood up, bracing his hands on the picnic table to swing one leg out from under it.

Ascupart grabbed the leg in mid-swing, pinching it between giant thumb and forefinger.

He squeezed and the calf muscle popped like a giant boil, the bone snapping with a rifle-shot *crack!* Then like a sick child torturing a pet kitten, he twisted the leg out of its socket with a wet ripping which was partly the sound of denim and partly of flesh being torn apart.

Stokes screamed, a high pitched, animal sound of pure agony. Still standing on his remaining leg, still bracing himself on the table top, he screamed and stared at the blood jetting out of the ragged stump.

"You cunt!" Gasman Tim yelled, and threw his empty pint at the monster's blood splattered face.

The only effect that the glass thudding against the vast visage had was to gain its attention.

The head turned to look at him, like the moon spinning on its axis.

It winked.

Then Ascupart took a playful nip.

A nip that bit through Tim's head.

Teeth plunged down through the top of Gasman Tim's scalp and up under his chin and snapped together through his skull.

When Ascupart drew away, Gasman's face was gone, crunched off, as if the young man had pushed his face into a guillotine and the blade had dropped. Like an anatomy illustration, the secret whorls of his sinuses were revealed, as well as the wagging stump of his tongue, and half his brain... which slopped out onto the table like a giant greasy turd.

Stokes was still standing, still screaming, still spraying blood.

Ascupart backhanded him twenty feet across the pub garden, to smash broken necked and suddenly silenced against a wall.

Gideon giggled.

Ascupart slowly turned to the sound.

Gideon giggled again as a single eye the size of his own face, blood red, focussed on him.

In his stoned state, he felt the things mind brush his. In Gideon's private ocean, he paddled over unthinkable depths... and something had risen from the fathomless darkness of the abyss beneath him, vaster than a whale.

And it was *gleeful*.

"Hello," said Gideon in a croaking whisper.

Ascupart grinned. Parts of Gideon's friends were claggy between the densely packed and cluttered butcher knives of its teeth.

Almost gently, it wrapped its hand around the young man's shoulders and picked him up.

Gideon giggled again, and felt his bowels void themselves. Sour diarrhoea oozed down his left leg as Ascupart held him up, tilted back its head, mouth opened wide, and extended the slimy coffin lid of its forked tongue to provide a slide for Gideon to glide down its gullet and into the hot, dark Hell of its already crowded belly.

Ascupart felt the mind of the genetic material trying to understand its final moments of consciousness, strange words attached to images of things he knew nothing of.

Hot tub - butcher shop - my friends.

Then; pure, sweet, screaming horror.

Ascupart closed its eyes and savoured.

There was still a glowing nearby.

Zena had kept very quiet under the table she had crawled beneath, shivering with shock as she saw her friends killed.

A thought kept going around in her head. A thought that was a delayed reaction to what she had seen as it had crawled up the terraces towards them, its back plainly visible before it was suddenly on top of them.

Why does it have WINGS?

Then the red eyes of the grey thing opened, that enormous almost-face towering above, and looked straight at her.

*****

What should have been an easy shift started with a dying man and nonsense.

PC Sunak and PC Moores hadn't been in the car together more than five minutes before they got a call to investigate a possible disturbance at the new building site at the top end of Bevois Valley.

"More flats, more students," sneered PC Moores.

PC Sunak, driving, nodded. Though the partners were from disparate cultural backgrounds, they shared plenty of the same opinions.

"Those were some beautiful old Georgian places," said PC Sunak, referring to the terraced houses that had been levelled along with the small scrub of ancient woodland. He sighed. "More kids earning more nonsense degrees in nonsense and getting so drunk they have to get stomach pumped."

PC Moores nodded. He briefly thought about Jack; he was coming up to university age, but he sure as shit wasn't going to be swanning off to some jumped up ivory tower somewhere and study for a BA in Socialist Feminazi Media Studies or some kind of bollocks.

Mind you, the kid didn't seem to have a mind to do anything with his life yet, hanging around with freaks and losers... No ambition, not like his old man, who wasn't planning on being a beat copper the rest of his career.

He just needed an opportunity to prove that he was detective material.

The call had been anonymous, somebody wanting something done but not wanting to get involved, as usual.

They pulled up at the Bevois Hill side of the building site, next to a small billboard that said *FUTURE SITE OF MORTGLAY PLACE*, along with an artist's watercolour depiction of what the development would look like. Their headlights revealed the gaping hole in the fence which had been cut through.

"It'll be kids," said PC Moores. "Fucking about."

"More than likely," said PC Sunak. "And long gone."

"Or..." PC Moores tapped his chin with the side of his thumb, thinking. "Any pikeys parked up locally?"

PC Sunak shook his head.

"Not that I've heard."

Travellers often passed through Southampton, setting up overnight in any unguarded car park on the industrial estates, or on the few playing fields that hadn't been sold off. New building sites were a favourite place for them to steal from, carrying off everything from pallets of cement and aggregates right through to heavy plant.

"'Mortglay Place'? What kind of stupid name is that?" sneered PC Moores.

"It's what the cheese grater really is," said PC Sunak.

"How's that?" Moores didn't ask his partner what he was referring to; the modern sculpture that had been erected at the top end of the Valley was a local joke of long standing. Everyone called it the cheese grater.

"You know the Valley is named after a mythical knight? Sir Bevis of Hamtun? Mortglay was the name of his magical sword."

"Yeah? Bit like King Arthur and Excalibur?"

"Yes. According to story, at the end of his life Sir Bevis stood upon the height of Arundel Tower and threw Mortglay as hard as he could, declaring he wished to be buried wherever the sword touched the ground. The cheese grater is supposed to represent the sword, Mortglay."

PC Moores snorted.

"Sunny, mate, you really are a mine of useless information." He shook his head and chuckled. "Fairy tales at your age..."

His partner shrugged. He'd been transferred to Southampton from Leicester five years before after he had played a part in breaking a grooming ring that had a number of respected Sikh business men amongst its members; the local community had ostracised him and his family, and a change of location was called for. Researching his new home's history was a hobby that had given him a sense of grounding. He'd even read the medieval romance called *Sir Bevis of Hamtun*, a fourteenth century epic of bloodshed and betrayal that seemingly no-one else in the whole city were even aware of.

They parked up and got out, each carrying a torch. PC Sunak called in that they were at the scene and investigating, and then they made their way through the gap in the fence.

There wasn't much to scene, just hillocks and divots of ploughed earth, the first stages of clearing the site ready for foundations to go in and work to begin in earnest.

"Quick back and forth yeah?" said PC Moores. "Like you said, more than likely they've long gone..."

"There."

PC Sunak's torch beam had fallen on something ten yards off.

When they got closer they saw it was a moped.

It was lying on its side, seemingly sunken into the ground, as if it had been lying there when there had been heavy rain and sank into mud which had now turned firm again.

Except it hadn't been raining lately.

"Very strange," said PC Sunak, tracing his beam over the vehicle. He handed his torch to PC Moores and bent down at the mopeds rear end, pulling his notepad from his pocket. "It looks like it's been... *pressed* into the ground. Like a steam roller rolled over it. I'll get the plates and we'll run them back at the car."

To get at the rear registration he had to dig a little with his free hand.

PC Moores had already put the story together in his head. Nicked bike, kids pissing around, their own private dirt track for the evening... Was there some kind of earth flattening plant around here that they'd then run over the bike with after they'd gotten bored?

He was keeping one torch beam trained where his partner was digging away clods and was lazily scanning the other back and forth across the rest of the site. Aside from the tyres tracks of the lorries and trucks which had been here to take away the rubble of the flattened buildings and the trunks and foliage of the pathetic bit of woodland that had been there, he could clearly see the skid marks left behind by a moped being ridden to near-destruction.

It was on the third sweep that he picked out the second object.

"Sunny," said PC Moores. "Body."

PC Sunak looked up.

PC Moores was already calling for an ambulance when they reached the prone figure.

White male, anywhere from late fifties to early eighties... still breathing, a wheezing, rattling sound.

PC Sunak had the more advanced emergency response training. He quickly went over the older man's body, checking for his vitals, relaying his findings to his partner who passed them to the dispatcher.

"On its way," said PC Moores. Then; "Jesus, they've beaten him half to death."

"I'll need the kit from the car," said PC Sunak, turning to head back to the fence. "I think he's bleeding internally."

PC Moores nearly rolled his eyes, as if the little green bag of first aid shit they kept was going to do much for the poor fucker. Anyone could see at least two, three, who knew how many thugs had been laying the boot in.

He knew he shouldn't move him, so he still squatted down and started talking to the old boy instead, reassuring him that help was coming.

The older man opened his eyes.

PC Moores started.

Jesus, you're an ugly cunt aren't you? he thought. *Were your parents cousins or something?*

The old boy opened his mouth.

He said something, croaked it, a trio of odd and unrelated syllables.

"Take it easy," said PC Moores. "An ambulance is on its way. Looks like you've been in the wars."

The lined and beaten face moved its mouth again, and again croaked those same three syllables.

"Arse cute part?" PC Moores tried fitting words to the sounds. "Sir, please conserve your strength, you've been assaulted, but help is here and medical aid will be with us any minute."

The old boy's face suddenly contorted into a look of rage, and PC Moores had a flashback to his schooldays, to Mr Simmonds the maths teacher, a brutal bastard who lost his temper easily with students who could not grasp what to him was as clear as day.

"*He's loose!*" hissed the beaten man through split and bloody lips.

"Calm yourself please, sir, a medical team needs to examine you so..."

"*He's loose!*" hissed the old man again, his washed out blue, bloodshot eyes bulging wild as he struggled to get up, though his inured body wouldn't let him. "*Free at last! Free again! A thousand years of hunger!*"

PC Moores gently but firmly pushed the beaten man back down again and tried to hold him steady. Who knew what kind of internal injuries he might have, bleeding that could be aggravated by his thrashing.

"Please sir, please remain calm and stay down!"

"*Free! Free to feed! Free to eat and eat and eat...*"

The old man continued to rave, struggling against PC Moores's attempts to keep him in place until the ambulance crew arrived, but whatever he was saying suddenly faded away like the volume was turned down.

PC Moores had placed the torch to one side as he had struggled with the older man, laying it on the ground so that its beam only lit the scene at an oblique angle the policeman didn't want it blazing straight in his or the victim's face.

He'd turned his head to see if Sunny was heading back across the uneven dirt ground yet, and that's when he glimpsed what the torch's beam was now illuminating.

Bodies.

Or parts of, at least.

Scraps, thought PC Moores... then wondered. *Scraps? What the fuck made me think of that word?*

Then;

Jesus. Jesus CHRIST....

Somebody sighed. A long, wheezing, very tired sound.

PC Moores looked down.

The old boy had died.

*****

"GO on, it really pisses her off," said Astra.

Jack didn't frown, but only because he rarely made any sort of facial expression.

"Why would I want to piss her off?" he asked.

"Because it's funny! Shh, shut up, here she is, do it."

The single member of bar staff had come down to where they were stood, raising safety pin pierced eyebrows in bored enquiry, folding her arms across a black t-shirt with the pub's name on it, *The Hobbit,* written in Olde English lettering.

"Yeah?"

"We would like to buy drinks," said Jack.

The barmaid blinked heavily kohled eyes.

Jack didn't elaborate.

Astra kept a straight face. She loved it when people met her boyfriend for the first time.

When it was clear he wasn't going to follow up, the barmaid asked, "What do you want?"

"Drinks," said Jack.

Astra made a stifled hiccupping sound.

The barmaid's expression had moved from bored to pissed off.

"Are you having a bubble? *What* drinks?"

"Oh," said Jack. He recognised the colloquialism, a piece of rhyming slang. Bubble bath; laugh. She was asking him if he was being serious, because the social convention was to state what *kind* of drinks he wanted to purchase.

He glanced up to the cocktail menu written in multi-coloured chalk on the huge blackboard hanging above the optics behind the bar. Astra has instructed him to purchase something not listed there, which was confusing, but she had said it was listed as something else. "One pint of lemonade, and a... Smeagol."

The barmaid's expression shifted again, but this time tilting back towards bored, shot through with contempt.

"Ha." She said. "Ha. Ha. Such sparkling and original wit."

She turned and stalked back down the length of the empty bar to start mixing the drink.

Astra started laughing, and ignored the look of disgust that was shot at her.

"Can you explain the joke?" asked Jack. "The drink isn't called that, and I might be on the spectrum but even I could tell that her response was clearly sarcasm."

Astra flapped her hand in front of her face.

"The pub's called The Hobbit, right?" she said. Jack nodded. "So the cocktail menu up there is all names from those books, Lord of the Rings, right?

That's the gimmick, instead of calling them Mojitos or Pina Coladas they call them a Gandalf, a Legolas, a Sauron, and so on."

"I am following your reason so far. The drinks are themed."

Astra sighed and rolled her eyes.

"Yes. But... did you ever see the films? Or read the books?"

Jack shook his head. He disliked fiction. It was ridiculous, following rules and conventions that bore no semblance to life as he understood it; reality was unstructured chaos.

"Well, one of the characters is called Gollum..."

"Like the drink you wanted."

"Yeah..."

"But you had me ask for a Smeagol."

"Yes!" Astra said. "Shut up! Because his name used to be Smeagol before he found the One Ring and got corrupted and turned into Gollum... and people who come in here thinking they're clever asking for a Smeagol instead of a Gollum are too stupid to realise that loads of other dickheads have come in thinking up the exact same clever thing, which is why everyone who works here gets pissed off..." Astra trailed off. "And you aren't following why it's funny are you?"

"No," said Jack.

Astra searched her boyfriend's eyes and face for any glimmer that he had connected the dots.

No.

She'd always been attracted to weirdoes, but Jack was almost alien in the way he didn't understand the simplest forms of human interaction. On the spectrum? Yeah, like infra-fucking-red was on the spectrum.

But he was pretty, and he went down on command.

And he's fucking good at it, like he's had a lot of practice...

A fleeting thought.

"Lemonade." A pint glass thumped the sticky wooden bar, ice cubes rattling. "Gollum." A half-pint glass full of something green and fizzy. "Enjoy."

The barmaid turned and headed back down to the other end of the bar where she resumed reading a Six Sigma manual

"Fucking dead in here," said Astra, sipping her drink. "Come on, the crew will all be out back."

She held out her hand. Jack could do this part; she'd trained him. He took it, and together they walked down the stairs that lead to the beer garden.

When they emerged outside, the first thing that hit them both was the smell of opened bodies, drifting up to them from further down the stepped slope. The smell was even strong enough to override the usual pervading stench of the toilets, which were themselves a legend in the mythology of the city's nightlife.

"Jesus fuck, what stinks?" asked Astra, letting go of Jack's hand to cup a palm over her nose.

Jack at first couldn't tell whether this was supposed to be rhetorical or not. One of his difficulties was telling when people genuinely meant to ask questions they wanted answers too, especially when the answers were readily apparent.

In this case, it was obvious what the origin of the smell was. It was squatting barely twenty feet away from them, something from a nightmare.

Astra finally focussed her attention from her immediate olfactory impression to the visual, and screamed a question that, again, Jack felt must have been a rhetorical one.

"*What the fuck is that?*"

And even though Jack Moores had never gotten the script that every other human seemed to have, he knew what the line here was.

"A monster," he said.

Ascupart was squatting in a nest of debris, of broken benches and tables and body parts. One hand rested in its lap, limp, and the other was raised in front of its huge, round face. This hand had a single finger extended straight upward like someone who was examining something they had rooted from their nose, and on that finger, impaled from vagina to mouth, was Astra's friend Zena.

Her legs and arms twitched. Her eyes rolled.

Ascupart was staring at her, fascinated.

It paid no attention to the two human's who had just emerged from the pub. Its red eyes seemed slightly glazed, and fixed entirely on the dancing piece of meat it had impaled.

The tip of its bloody finger was sticking out of Zena's mouth. Her jaw had dislocated to accommodate it. Her legs were sticking out at harsh angles over Ascupart's knuckles, blood dribbling from her split vagina.

Astra was panting, her heart racing.

"What is it?" she whispered. "What is it Jack? What the fuck is that thing?"

Jack had already answered that question.

"We should leave," he told her.

Ascupart looked at them. It blinked its huge red eyes slowly. A foolish grin gradually unsheathed bloody teeth.

Then it looked back at the girl-kebab.

Asupart shook his hand.

Zena's arms flapped from side to side.

"Zena," said Astra. "That's Zena oh fuck is she still *alive?*"

The monster made a noise that sounded like a huge and rusty engine turning over but failing to start up.

Jack had a sudden intuition into the impossible nightmare before them. Whilst the nuances of every day social interactions were a continuing source of bafflement to him, he often had insights and epiphanies and leaps of reasoning which most people could never make, as their minds were too inclined to make narratives that made sense.

"It's stoned," he said.

It shook its hand again, wagging its finger left and right and making Zena's arms flap back and forth, a puppet with the strings cut. Again, like some huge engine failing to start, it made a bass deep noise both Jack and Astra felt in their guts.

"Laughter," said Jack.

Astra moaned.

Ascupart curled its finger and Zena's body split in half as if it were a chrysalis and the finger was an emerging caterpillar that had failed to metamorphose into a butterfly, ripping open the cocoon of muscle and bone from crotch to throat, ribs and lungs bursting out of her chest, liver and intestine spurting out of her belly as the skin split like tissue paper.

The sundered corpse slid down the back of Ascupart's now closed fist and slumped to the debris strewn ground.

Then it looked back at the young couple, still stood holding hands and staring at it. It slowly blinked its huge red eyes... and finally seemed to see them.

Neither Jack nor Astra moved.

"We really should leave," said Jack.

"It's looking at me," said Astra.

"Yes, that's why I think we should leave," said Jack.

"It's looking at *me*," moaned Astra.

The monster's eyes had narrowed slightly, and Jack realised that his girlfriend was correct, that the centre of its attention had shifted to her in particular.

For this he was glad. In the space of only the minute or so they had been exposed to the giant, he had felt his mind grind against its own, a piece of pumice being crushed under a boulder of granite... and he had *seen*.

Jack did not think like other people. It was because of this that his own consciousness grinding against something so utterly alien had allowed him to glean a lot of information.

He saw everything.

Like a film, a long film, an entire trilogy, running at a thousand times the speed it should, the *thing's* mind the projector and his own the screen it played out on.

What it was, where it had come from... what was going to happen.

If he had thought like most people he would have gone insane by what he learned. Instead, he accepted it as he accepted the seemingly inexplicable behaviour of his own species.

Ascupart's rudimentary features gave the impression it was thinking.

And then it spoke.

"EEE IIII OOO MMM... SSDDAARRRRR..."

It voice was guttural, barely a voice at all, more like the sound of shifting rubble.

Astra moaned again.

"It knows my name."

Jack did something he had never done before in his short relationship with the girl. Or, indeed, *ever* in his life.

He took charge.

"We're going," he said, and dragged her back inside the pub.

*****

Ascupart watched the DNA sources go.

The flesh it had consumed this night had been drugged, it seemed, the blood of the food at the burying place saturated with the same chemicals as the food it had consumed here. And more; some of the little ones had survived long enough for their minds to be digested in a way quite different to their flesh. The memories of that genetic material –the one which thought of itself as CUNT FACE, and that other that knew itself as GIDEON- had become Ascupart's memories, mixed in with the centuries of stored experiences from past meals.

Ascupart squatted amongst the carnage it had wrought and, after its own fashion, thought.

The CUNT FACE memories had recognised the food that had fled... Ascupart had named that food because it could, because it was dimly amusing to feel its terror at being named. But the GIDEON memories had been thinking of something that was interesting.

There was to be gathering in some other part of the city. Many, many little ones were due to gather in a single place.

The WEST QUAY.

Stirring itself, Ascupart gained its feet and blundered forth.

*****

The slaughter was an opportunity, and PC Moores was not going to let standard procedure or even decency prevent him from grasping it.

In the minutes between Sunny getting back from the car with the now useless first aid kit and the first ambulance arriving, Moores had made his case.

This was big, he said. Huge. A fucking massacre. Probably a dust up between rival drugs gangs, or more likely some firm from outside the city who wanted to make an impression on the local boys. And they were first on the scene! This was their chance at doing some serious fucking police work, make their names... as long as they didn't let CSI swoop in and take over, like they were bound to do as soon as they got a sniff, you and me Sunny, we've got perhaps an hour of two before the shit really hits the fan to get our foot stuck in the door so they can't shut us out...

PC Sunak was only half-listening. He had seen the *scraps* and, after being professional and calling in the new information of multiple fatalities, had vomited.

"...but where do we go from here? The old boy doesn't have any ID on him, no witnesses... Shit," mused PC Moores. He paused, and then, mostly to himself; "Arse cute part."

Wiping his lips clean of the half-digested Big Mac he had snatched before starting his shift, PC Sunak fixed on his partner's last few words.

"What was that?" he asked.

PC Moores was frowning at the cooling body between them, but his torch was focussed on the mess of torn flesh and bones that lay just yards away, as if he were afraid that should he switch the light off they would vanish and with them his *chance*.

"Arse cute part. Those were the old boy's last words."

PC Sunak spat a partially digested fragment.

"Ascupart?"

PC Moores looked up from the corpse, one eyebrow cocked.

"Yeah... yeah, that's what he said. Ascupart, yeah. You know what it means, Sunny?"

"It's a name," said PC Sunak. "It was the name of the giant that Sir Bevis brought back with him."

"How's that?"

"Sir Bevis of Hamtun," said PC Sunak. "Like I was telling you. In the stories he was said to have brought a giant back from the middle east, a giant called Ascupart. He brought him back from Mount Ararat in Armenia."

PC Moores grimaced.

"Fuck's sake, more fairy tales."

"But it's also the name of those flats over there," said PC Sunak, pointing towards the far side of the building site. "Ascupart House."

PC Moores felt his heart trip over its own feet. Fucking hell, it had been a clue, and it was within spitting distance...

Sirens were approaching.

The window of opportunity was closing.

"Sunny mate, do the right thing, cover for me," he said, and before his partner could protest the gross breach of protocol, he was making for the road.

As PC Moores ducked through the gap in the fence the sensible voice in his head was telling him that he was looking at a disciplinary for this; abandoning his partner at the scene of a major incident in order to chase glory.

He stifled that voice.

He glimpsed flashing blue lights approaching from the bottom end of the Valley.

Now or never.

He jogged up Bevois Hill to the crossroads where it met Portswood Road, Lodge Road, and Thomas Lewis Way. Traffic lights cycled through their colours for no passing traffic, a dead night. The little snack and fuel sat-nav in his head reminded him there was an Esso garage and a Tesco Express about fifty yards down Lodge, but what he wanted was on the other side.

Opposite where he stood was a flat roofed apartment building that looked a little like a castle, if you were of a fanciful bent of mind. It was higher than the road, set behind a brick wall and a hedge, flanked by trees down the Portswood Road side, with a cycle path leading up onto the pavement; the first floor had brick balconies, and there were lights behind the curtains of half of the visible windows.

He jogged across the road, then up the gentle gradient of the pavement to a short set of switch back stairs with metal railings. On the wall of the first landing was a blue plaque about the size of a street sign, with white lettering that read;

ASCUPART HOUSE.

Arse cute part... the old boy had to have lived here. Made sense; probably heard the noise the sods with the stolen moped were making and decided to go down and play Neighbourhood Watch.

And got kicked to death for his trouble.

...except that doesn't explain the

(scraps)

other bodies does it? The ones that look like they've been torn apart.

That was the same voice that had told him, rightly, that leaving Sunny at the scene to deal with the shit show that was about to start was a really bad fucking idea... a voice that he often heard when his hand was on the handle of his son's bedroom door, telling him this was wrong, wrong, wrong.

PC Moores snuffed it.

He'd had plenty of practice.

...and what do you know, opening the door of the apartment building and negating the need to systematically try the buzzer of each individual flat until someone let him in, here was an old biddy who was looking worried, as if her husband had gone out to give some louts a piece of his mind and hadn't returned yet.

Poor cunt, thought PC Moores. But his heart beat a little faster. Every connection he made, every piece of information he could glean, would wedge his foot in the door a little firmer when CSI tried to slam it closed.

He let his face turn as blank as his conscience, as blank as a whitewashed wall. Every copper knew the trick; give away nothing, let them give to you.

The old biddy was at least two heads shorter than him, with an owlish face and very thin white hair that came down to her shoulders. She wore a huge purple kaftan wrapped around her shoulders, and the first words out of her mouth were; "Is Ascupart awake?"

*****

Despite the fear that was making her heart drum as fast as she wished she could walk, Charmaine was elated, knowing she was going to be free, hoping that everything was going to be alright, and oh if the poor girl had learned anything in her shitty and soon-to-be-over life, she should have known not to dare hope.

But as she waddled towards her end, she did dare.

Fuck you Simon, she thought, hitching her bag up higher on her shoulder with one hand, the other cradling the huge swell of her belly. She giggled; until this evening, she wouldn't have dared to even think those words.

And now she had thought them...

"Fuck you Simon!" she shouted in the street, and giggled again, bubbling laughter that was close to hysteria.

She carried everything that she could gather in a rush, bits of clothing and toiletries stuffed willy-nilly into a Sport Direct bag-for-life, but none of the baby stuff. She'd been in such a hurry that she had thought, *I'm going to need food*, and ended up jamming a half empty box of Coco Pops in with the pregnancy bras and roll-on deodorants. She could hear the cereal rustling as she walked, and as she made her way down Denzil Avenue heading for Onslow Road where she had vague plans to flag down a taxi and have it take her to her mum's flat over in Lordshill to finally give up her pride, she realised that Simon would have nothing to eat when he got up for breakfast. He always had his bowl of Coco Pops with soy milk and a cup of Typhoo One Cup tea, as sure as every Tuesday night he expected a baked potato and fish fingers for his dinner with half-and-half garden peas and sweetcorn, and God help Charmaine if she dared suggest any other kind of meal plan for a change... and in her frightened, joyous, adrenaline fuelled state of mind this struck her as hysterically funny.

Her laughter was too much, she had to stop.

She leant against one of the parked cars that lined by sides of the street bumper to bumper and giggled quietly. She wanted to roar, but three years with Simon meant everything she did was quiet. Too much noise upset him.

Charmaine let the bag drop to the pavement. She squatted carefully, her belly threatening to overbalance her, and rummaged until she found the cereal.

She stood up.

With great dignity, she managed to suppress her giggles, and solemnly poured the chocolate flavoured puffed rice onto the ground, as if pouring a libation to the Gods.

"We'd rather have a bowl of Coco Pops," she sang, quietly, and giggled again.

In her belly, one of the twins shifted, an arm or a leg adjusting for comfort.

She stopped giggling. Fear was uppermost again, suppressing the hysteria.

Her babies.

Simon slept lightly. His body clock would be expecting her in bed not long after him, after she had finished tidying the wreckage of the living room. About now, actually. He could already be turning over and wondering why her bulk wasn't resting silently next to him. Then he'd get up and go downstairs and discover that the living room was still a war zone, and that not only had his wife not tidied up after his rampage, but had also done the unthinkable and walked out...

He'd been in a good mood, she'd thought. He'd come in and kissed her as she stood waiting for him at the door... just like always. Then, just like always, she had fetched his dinner for him as he settled onto the sofa to watch the news like he did every evening after work. Fish fingers and a baked potato, served with garden peas and sweetcorn mixed fifty-fifty; it was Tuesday, after all.

Charmaine had already eaten, of course. Simon hated the way she ate, too noisy, fork tines scratching the plate and mashing separate elements of the food together instead of eating them one by one... and so she ate separately to him. She'd just sat on the sofa, watching him eat all the peas and sweetcorn first before her ate the baked potato, before moving onto the five fish fingers which he ate last, cutting each into three pieces before eating them one by one.

To say Simon Orne was a creature of habit would be an understatement. To say he was a control freak would be more accurate. But this was what had drawn her to him in the first place; having grown up with a succession of "uncles" as her mum had chopped and changed the various boyfriends, fiancés, and casual lodgers who had lived with them during Charmaine's childhood and adolescence, she had always hungered for a staid, stable, predictable relationship.

After he'd finished his food she took his plate away and asked him about his day.

He told her to shut up.

Charmaine had shut up. His tone was familiar, more and more familiar as the months had passed and her belly had grown, and sent icy insects scuttling up her back.

"Are you sure you really want kids?" he had asked her. His tone was casual. He was staring at the television, and the television was off.

The insects became a swarm.

"Of course," said Charmaine. "Yeah, of course I do. Babes, I'm due in three weeks, what do you mean do I really want kids?"

Simon nodded, still staring at the blank screen as if it were a scrying mirror in which he could see their future.

"We wouldn't be able to go on holiday this year," he said.

They went to an apartment complex in Chania, in Crete, every year. Simon had gone there with his parents every year since he was six, and hadn't missed a year in the previous twenty.

"But we'd be able to go again next year, just like always," said Charmaine. "But we'd be a family. It would become our family holiday, just like you and your mum and dad used to."

He nodded, still gazing at the future in the blank screen.

All he could see was disruption.

Charmaine had known he'd been getting moodier as the pregnancy had gone on, but he'd not had a rage since...since the scan showing they were expecting twin boys, and he'd already decorated the nursery for one child.

She'd thought when they were born, things would be different.

"I've been looking at cars," said Simon.

"Yeah?"

He nodded.

"Going to need a new car," he said. "My old Fiesta won't do the job, not with two babies and all the shopping we're going to have to do. Going to have to write new shopping lists as well."

On Charmaine's backs, the insects with frozen feet had stopped moving. They were fluttering wings made of frost, chilling her blood.

"I'll have to make some adjustments in our budget," said Simon. "To be able to afford all the new things on the new shopping lists. Which means we'll have to cut back on some other things. Re-balance. Like, no more cinema trip on the second Sunday of the month; and no more Chinese takeaway every Bank Holiday Monday."

The Happy Wok, one order of spring rolls to share, satay vegetables and chicken balls for him, beef chow mein for me, thought Charmaine, automatically.

And on the heels of that; *Oh fuck me.*

Simon had patted the arm of the sofa with one palm.

"Get out," he said softly.

Even if the last rage had been months ago, Charmaine was still pre-conditioned.

She got up and left the room quickly, and then Simon proceeded to silently trash the place.

He was silent, anyway; it was everything else that made noise. He didn't scream or swear or shout or make any sound himself, just the pictures and ornaments he smashed and shattered against the walls.

After he was done, he said he was tired and he was going to bed.

Halfway up the stairs, he had turned and asked her again;

"Are you sure you really want kids?"

But he hadn't waited for an answer.

Charmaine had listened to the sounds of him getting ready for bed, standing in the middle of the living room.

When she heard the bed creaking as her husband climbed into his side of it, she had one very clear thought.

She had a quick glimpse of the future. It was like watching a TV program.

In this vision, Simon pushed her down the stairs. The stairs were quite sharp, and they hurt like hell as she tumbled arse over head down them, feeling two ribs break, feeling the thumb on her right hand snap, her forehead bouncing off the second to last step, finally coming to rest at the bottom, her huge belly now looking oddly distorted as if the contents had been punched into new shapes and feeling sudden hot wetness flooding between her legs...

The vision was very vivid, very detailed.

And so she had left, grabbed the Sports Direct bag-for-life from one of a half dozen they kept by the front door for doing the weekly shop with, filled it with whatever came to hand that she thought she might need to start her life afresh on the spur of the moment, and walked out.

Walked out on her marriage and the prison which she had deluded herself into thinking was her home.

Or waddled out, anyway. Being pregnant with twins made moving at any speed faster than a hippo with sprained ankles utterly impossible... but now she was within sight of a main road where she knew taxis passed regularly, and she was going to wave one down and have it take her back to her mum's, where she would have to swallow her pride and admit that her warning about Simon from years before was entirely correct.

He's a wrong 'un, had been her mum's initial opinion, and she hadn't changed it, save for variations whenever Charmaine advanced her relationship; moving in together, getting married, getting pregnant... *There's something up with him, gives me the heeby-jeebies. Wouldn't trust him as far as I could throw him if both me arms were broken. Have you SEEN the way he eats, what sort of a bloke eats like that, a bloke with more loose screws than B&Q, that's what sort...*

Just please don't gloat, Charmaine thought, still leaning against the car and staring at the scattered breakfast cereal on the pavement.

What would have followed next would have been the doubts. She was only a few hundred yards from home. The nesting instinct would have kicked in, and all those elements of denial that had established and then built a relationship with Simon in the first place, coupled with memories of all the good qualities he had that she had told herself she had fallen in love with.

But none of this happened because before the doubts could muster their attack on her resolve, she heard something.

Heard and felt it, under her feet.

Thundering, a heavy weight falling and striking the ground repeatedly, like footfalls, only huge.

Footsteps. Running footsteps.

Too big to be human.

For some reason, she thought of an elephant stampeding.

She turned her head and saw the nightmare pounding towards her.

It was running down the centre of the street, its bulk taking up the entire gap between the cars parked solidly end-to-end on either side of the road. Its gaze was upon her.

And it was grinning.

Charmaine had another little glimpse of the future, much like the vision in which she had seen her husband push her down the stairs to snuff the lives she carried.

Fee fi fo fum...

Very vivid, very detailed, she saw everything that was to come.

If she'd had a gun she would have broken her teeth getting it into her mouth fast enough to blast out her brains to make sure that future never happened.

The giant slowed its run as it saw that its prey was frozen in place. His footsteps cracked the already abused tarmac as he plodded the rest of the distance towards the next source of DNA.

Charmaine felt hot swetness flood between her legs.

She had pissed herself, or her water's had broken.

Too late to matter either way.

Grinning, grinning, Ascupart smashed aside the rank of parked cars in front of where Charmaine stood like they were empty boxes, doors buckling inwards and windows exploding into false diamonds.

I'm like a rabbit in headlights, thought Charmaine.

Yes, like some dumb animal crossing a road that freezes solid when its doom bears down on it doing sixty. Neither fight nor flight, just terror that roots it to the spot where in moments it will become a smear of fur and guts.

The giant loomed over her.

Charmaine had no frame of reference, as this was both the first and last time she would witness it, but in the scant hours of his rebirth, Ascupart had undergone a metamorphosis. His proportions had changed from a foetus to a baby, and now to something like a toddler.

He was growing up.

And like all growing boys, he was ravenous.

He paused, his breath stinking of burst bodies wafting down on the terrified woman.

His mind was brushing more than one *other*.

The female thing called CHARMAINE glowed fiercely, burning bright with terror. But there were other, dimmer glows within her...

He picked her up, one huge hand wrapped around her body. His fingers felt the different shape of her; she was much rounder in the middle than the night's other food had been.

Inside the roundness were the other glows.

Charmaine found herself being lifted towards the eyes, and in her final seconds, she found she could pray.

Please God, she asked silently, the breath being crushed from her preventing her asking aloud from the light-polluted heavens above. *Just don't let it hurt.*

Of course, nothing was listening.

Ascupart, intrigued, squeezed.

Charmaine gasped.

Her brain supplied a memory as its final act.

She remembered her grandparents house in Eastleigh. She remembered helping her grandpa harvest peas on his little allotment. She recalled helping her grandmother shell them for dinner, squeezing the pods until they squirted the tiny green vegetables.

The giant's fingers pressed tightest on her belly. The relentless strength pushed her womb inside out, and her cunt split open to her anus as her babies gushed forth and splattered in a welter of blood and membranes onto the filthy, cracked pavement nine feet below her dangling legs.

Ascupart tilted his head.

The glows had flared brightly as they emerged into the world.

Impressions from unformed minds;

LIGHT-AIR-SPEED-LOSS-COLD-PAIN...

With the clumsy fingers of his free hand, he stooped and scraped one of the glows up off the ground.

He held it up to inspect.

A tiny face, eyes tightly closed, trying to summon breath for its first cry of outrage at this awful new condition of dryness and air and cold, so removed from the warm, wet darkness it had always known.

On the blunt end of his finger it looked like something he might have picked from his nose, if he had had one; squishy and bloody, as if he had rooted too deep.

And just like any dirty little boy who picked his nose, he popped it in his mouth.

Ascupart's tongue found the morsel, and was disappointed. Its mind lacked definition to give its death any true piquancy.

In fact, the only thing the baby felt before he chewed it was relief to be back in the warm, wet darkness again.

To show his displeasure, Ascupart stepped on the other newborn, and ground it into a smear before swallowing its mother whole.

Able to breathe again, she screamed all the way down. Perhaps, at the end, Charmaine Orne knew some good luck; her mouth wide open and howling, she choked and drowned before she realised *what* she was drowning in.

Ascupart took a moment to digest what she knew.

Nothing about the gathering at the WEST QUAY that the previous DNA sources hadn't known.

Not that it mattered; the giant had set this place as its destination, and not even the glows that were surrounding him now as people opened curtains or front doors —curtains and front doors that were closed rapidly as the house occupants saw what had been making the noise outside- were as tempting as the potential for acquiring genetic material it had encountered in the GIDEON'S mind.

Fee fi fo fum...

*****

Before she could invite the policeman inside and arm him with the stories he would need, his radio had buzzed.

He'd apologised, and stepped away out of earshot to have a spirited conversation with whoever had contacted him.

She'd waited.

She was sad, terribly sad, because she knew her brother must have been dead... after all, why else would the police have come?

Her brother had gone down to the burial place, and he had not come back, and now a policeman was here.

And that could only mean one thing.

After what looked to have been an intense conversation, the policeman had come back to the door and told her he was sorry but he had to go.

And left rapidly.

Which left her confused and bereft.

Watching the policeman run out of sight, heading back towards the burial ground, she had thought to call out to him, to tell him to come back...But she wasn't resolute or quick enough, and the opportunity was lost.

So she went back upstairs, to the flat.

Locked the door.

Still in shock, she stood in the living room of the flat for long minutes rubbing her hands together.

Then she wandered through to her brother's study.

It was a small room. It wasn't a big flat. The family fortune had dwindled over the centuries, shrinking even as the family line did. From controlling vast swathes of land and numbering in their dozens, a family of importance, a family of respect... to just the two of them, in this flat, as close to the burial ground as possible.

Brother and sister, the last of their line, keeping an eye on the place where the giant had fallen nearly a thousand years before.

This little room contained all the history. Ancient books written on vellum and parchment., treatise and diaries of their distinguished family, and also many other books written by other people which her brother had used to piece together the true story of the thing their family called Ascupart... *Chariots of the Gods, The Spaceships of Ezekiel, Technologies of the Gods*, and many others about "ancient astronauts."

She wasn't very bright. She knew she wasn't. She had never needed to be, her brother had handled their finances and day-to-day concerns; all that was expected of her was to have a baby and keep their family going, but she couldn't, and so she and her brother were the last.

Her brother hadn't been angry that she couldn't have his babies. But he had always impressed upon her the importance of their family's duty and history... even if she wasn't entirely clear on the details.

He'd told it to her as a simple story.

Once upon a time, angels came to Earth and had babies with humans. These babies became evil giants called Nephilim. So God sent a flood to destroy them. God told Noah to build a ship to carry two of every animal to survive the flood. Only one of the evil giants also survived by clinging onto the side of the ark...

Her brother had explained to her that these were all "metaphors".

"They weren't really angels, but because they were powerful and came down from the sky people called them that... and they didn't have babies like we mean babies, but tinkered with human DNA for their own purposes... and the ark wasn't really a ship like the container and the cruise ships you see down on the docks, but a different kind of ship, and there weren't really two of every animal on it, but their genetics..."

But no matter how many times he had tried to explain what the story in the Bible really meant, she was not able to grasp it.

...and then the man we call Sir Bevis found the evil giant in the wreckage of the ship on Mount Ararat... the evil giant had been trapped there for a long, long time, but he didn't die, he just sort of changed back into a baby, reverted... and there was this thing that myths call a sword that Bevis also found that could control the evil giant...

The magic sword! But it wasn't really a sword, it was a "metaphor".

And it was hanging on the wall of the little room, emitting an eerie glow and a gentle hum, as it had done for centuries as it was passed down through generations of their family.

She rubbed her hands compulsively.

Her brother was gone.

That meant she had to tell the stories to someone, and give them the sword, so they could stop the evil giant who wasn't really a giant, but something else... something worse.

But the policeman had gone away.

And now she was alone and didn't know what to do.

So she did nothing.

The last Lady Josian of the Bevis line turned and left her brother's study and left the thing that wasn't a sword just hanging there on the wall, glowing and humming and useless.

*****

His son was with the fat girl, the one with half a cutlery drawer shoved through her face, and this fact pissed him off almost as much as he was relieved to see his child alive.

I told him to stop wasting his time with that goth slag!

PC Moores' only offspring and his girlfriend and the two members of staff who were working that night were all gathered in the upstairs front bar area of The Hobbit. A couple of support officers were keeping an eye on them whilst more police were attempting to make sense of whatever had happened in the pub's beer garden.

What had happened?

Sunny had radioed him just as he had met the old biddy who'd mentioned that fairytale name again ("Is Ascupart awake?") and Moores might have played for time if it wasn't for what his partner had breathlessly relayed; a second massacre.

And Jack was there.

At first PC Moores blood had turned to rime and his balls had retracted up when he confused what his partner was saying. He'd heard "massacre" and his boy's name and...

No, no, Jack is there, at the pub, one of the witnesses. Alive. He saw what happened.

And this was what had sent him running back down towards the Valley, leaving the biddy in the kaftan at the door.

PC Sunak was at the centre of a lot of activity at the building site and looking well out of his depth. Two ambulances and three other police patrols were already there. Twirling blue lights and full beam headlights were attracting members of Joe Public to the scene, and Sunny had found himself the momentary ringmaster of the whole fucking circus.

"Where the blazes have you been?" hissed Sunny, dragging his partner into a loose huddle.

"Jack," was all Moores was able to say, breathless from sprinting back. "What about Jack?"

PC Sunak told his partner what he knew, which was just repeating what he had told him over the radio. Bar staff at The Hobbit had called 999 and reported quote "a fucking slaughter, dead, they're all dead" end quote. The dispatcher had made a snap decision based on the fact that a couple of patrolling officers had called in a number of suspected fatalities in the area only twenty minutes prior, and had sent out as many bodies as they could to both scenes, escalating both incidents.

Sunny had kept half an ear on the radio as he directed the redundant ambulance crews to where the (scraps) building site bodies were, and had overheard a responding officer at the pub identify one of his colleague's children there.

Senior officers were on their way, and hey, where are you going?

But PC Moores had no time to answer such an obvious fucking question. When he reached The Hobbit he had a stitch in his left side and felt like his lungs were stuffed with rags soaked in bleach.

But no matter how bad he felt, the officer standing guard at the pub's front entrance looked worse.

It was Des Lynch, a twenty-three year career plod who enjoyed boring the shit out of his partners with tales of when police work in Southampton *meant* something.

The older man's face was white and cheesey with shock, and his lips were slick with something.

PC Moores caught the scent of bile.

The useless old tosser's shoes were covered with puke.

His balls crawled up again.

Des Lynch's eyes were a little glazed, but he recognised his colleague, and waved him in.

Just as Moores stepped passed him, the older man put his hand on his shoulder.

"Don't go out the back," he advised.

(s*craps*)

He'd shoved through into the upstairs bar to see his son, alive, and relief had flooded through him... an instant before he spotted that fat goth slag Jack kept hanging around with.

"Jack, are you alright son?"

The boy's face didn't change. It rarely did, because there was something wrong with him.

"There was a monster," he said simply. "It killed my friends. And it's not going to stop."

The fat goth slag had been cuddled into Jack's chest, and when she looked up with red rimmed eyes she left half her make-up on his clothes.

"It... knew... my... name..." she sobbed.

*****

The police response to what happened in the Valley was a mess for a number of reasons, not least the fact that Southampton wasn't well known for murders, let alone whole scale butchery.

Another reason was that the central dispatch that handled 999 began receiving an awful lot of calls with a recurrent theme in those few dreadful hours of that dreary Tuesday evening.

Yet *another* reason was that a lot of resources were already deployed in another part of the city, quite removed from where the initial fatalities were reported... though if one of the call operators in central dispatch had plotted those thematically similar calls onto a map, they might have been interested to note that they formed an almost straight line heading towards that other part of town.

The main bulk of the city's constabulary were in fact on detail at a major event at West Quay, the consumer jewel in Southampton's capitalist crown.

Pinky Sikene had come to town, and the newest title in the multi-million selling book series *Miss Nobody, Sexorcist* was due for release at midnight.

As with other best-selling sensations that had come before *–The Da Vinci Code, Harry Potter, 50 Shades of Grey*- the books had grown from being simply stories to a fully fledged cultural phenomena. A "sexorcist" without a name, the eponymous Miss Nobody, travelled the world getting rid of intruders from the Otherlands by fucking them to extinction. Creatures from folklore were re-imagined as sexual dynamos, and the pornographic misadventures between them and the sexorcist were explicitly detailed.

An enormous fandom had rapidly arisen around the books, drawn from every layer of society, a loyal cult who put each new title in the series at the top of every best-seller list across the world; part of the reason Pinky Sikene's smut had enjoyed such a meteoric rise to popularity was because she sent her protagonist to every corner of the world, so that readers in Japan got hot under the collar reading about her "laying" *yokai* like the water-demon kappa and living dildo tsukumogami, whilst readers in Ireland could rub one out to her matching slits & tits with a banshee or being gang-banged by leprechauns.

Every new book was met with a mad clamouring by the millions who enjoyed the sexorcist "bumping" the things of the night, but last month the elusive Pinky Sikene sent out a message on social media declaring that the next book was also the last, and that she would be appearing for the first (and last) time in public to launch the final adventure at a midnight release in the city of her birth... Southampton.

A final *Miss Nobody, Sexorcist* book?

A public appearance by the notoriously publicity shy author herself?

The news went global, and as soon as the date of release was revealed, fans from all over the world booked their plane tickets and hotel reservations to Southampton.

...as did the rather vocal members of various hard-right Christian denominations who had long railed against what they saw as Satanically inspired smut, promising that they were going to picket and protest against this Godless filth.

So a crowd of thousands of fanatical *Miss Nobody* fans and several hundred militant Bible thumpers were all due to converge in one place at the same time, such was the situation that the city's police department had expected to deal with this evening, rather than reports of mass slaughter, and of dozens of crank calls about something monstrous plunging through the streets.

*****

Alana Laurie was shitting herself, both literally and metaphorically.

One brought on the other.

She was nervous, and the nerves had manifested as rotten bowels.

No, nervous wasn't the right word.

She was *terrified*.

Why did I ever agree to this? She asked herself, sat on the toilet in the cubicle of the Waterstone's staff toilet. Before she answered herself, another blast erupted from her guts, pebble-dashing the already well abused bowl. *Oh yeah, fistfuls of cash.*

But even though she'd made enough money from this gig to buy herself and her parents a house each (as well as an Aston Martin for her dad) if she had had some inkling of what it would eventually entail she might have had second thoughts.

Fucking Swainey! "Just show your face, that's all," he said, "Sign a couple of books for a few selected members of the crowd and that's it, you and I are off the hook forever!" There must be two thousand people out there!

Alana Laurie was better known to the world as Pinky Sikene. The problem was, she was not the author of the notorious and multi-million selling series of paranormal erotica, but was a model who had been paid to be the public face of Pinky Sikene.

The author herself did not exist.

The person who wrote the books was a bloke called Gavin Swainey, who had realised at the very start of becoming a household name that someone who was young, attractive, and big breasted would make a better public face for the brand then his ugly mug. And so Alana had been selected to pose for the posts on Pinky's social media channels, as well as providing pre-recorded interview material for the mainstream media outlets.

But nobody associated with *Miss Nobody* had realised just how successful the books would become. Obsessed fans relentlessly assaulted the author's various channels with DMs of explicit fan-mail, whilst the various factions of Holy Rollers who took offence to the sexualisation and glamorising of all things demonic provided a secondary onslaught of threats *against* and appeals *to* her immortal soul.

Gavin Swainey had grown to hate his own creation. He'd long ago handed over the actual writing of the books to a stable of ghost-writers, but finally he had decided enough was enough.

One final book; the sexorcist would finally come up against a foe she could not lay.

The end.

Pinky Sikene would appear for the first and last time in public to announce her retirement from writing, a big blow out farewell in the form of a midnight book release and (very limited) signing session.

And this was why Alana was expelling most of her intestinal lining into the staff toilets of West Quay's largest book shop.

She had peeked outside.

The entire shop had been given over to the event, everywhere stacks of books like *Miss Nobody The Mile-High Haunting*, *Miss Nobody & The Garden of Unearthly Delights*, *Miss Nobody & the*

Gnazi Gnomes of Gnikomson, and the shop was full of weirdoes in costumes... not just the entire shop, in fact, but the entire shopping mall was crammed with nearly a thousand of *Miss Nobody's* fans, almost all wearing outfits designed to resemble their favourite characters from the series.

And beyond the doors of the mall? Nearly two hundred protestors with placards and banners denouncing the author and all her works.

Half of them want to fuck me, and half of them want to set me on fire, thought Alana on seeing the hordes... and bolted for the toilets before her bowels gave way.

Someone knocked on the door. One of the book store staff. The store manager, the lady in charge tonight, built like a brick shit house with a face like a bulldog licking piss off a thistle.

"Are you quite alright Miss Sikene?"

No, but I will be.

"I'll be out in just a bit," she called back. "Just have to powder my nose."

"Please be prompt, then. You have an audience fairly champing at the bit out here!"

Alana listened until she heard footsteps going away.

And fuck you very much!

Then she pulled out a baggie of ket.

Just a couple of lines...

*****

Ascupart blundered into East park.

He met a drug dealer lurking beneath a broken lamp post.

He ate him.

Then he met some homeless people, nearly insensible on a park bench from sharing a bottle of spirits.

He ate them too.

A male prostitute servicing a regular client in a clearing behind some bushes.

Ascupart thought that one of the men was trying to eat the other. They didn't notice him, so engaged in the act were they. He decided to join in; he bit the head off the standing one who was being swallowed very slowly by the one kneeling down.

The one who was doing the eating was surprised when his client had an explosive death orgasm. Not being prepared for the sudden blast of spunk down his throat, he fell back on his haunches coughing. As he fell back he looked up and saw his client's head replaced by a fountain of gore, an impressive display owing to the body's elevated blood pressure...

...and looming behind the still standing, headless corpse gushing excited blood, something from Hell.

*****

He was almost sorry he killed her.

Almost.

Secure in his anonymity, Gavin Swainey, a previously unsuccessful writer who had created both Pinky Sikene and Miss Nobody as idle wank fantasies to make a bit of quick cash, wandered amongst the crowd of fairies and demons and other denizens of the metaphysical realms.

Me, he thought dreamily. *All these people, some of whom have travelled from the other side of the world... they're all here and dressed like fucking mongs because of ME!*

Trolls and undines, basilisks and tengus and Jersey devils thronged about, laughing and chatting and gossiping in a buzz of excitement.

And none of you know that the book you are chomping at the bit to get your mitts on is going to really, really, PISS YOU OFF!

The thought was getting him high in a way no drug he had tried or anything he had bought with the money his franchise had made ever had.

He knew his creations were beloved by millions —his bank account and numerous overseas properties spoke to that truth- but he had never really understood it. The books he'd written for quick money were more wildly successful than any of his serious work would ever be. The whole point of creating the pseudonym was to keep what he perceived as worthless shit at artist-arm's length.

Hiring Alana the model had been part and parcel of that; a pretty face to slap on the books that would shift a few more copies as well as dissociate him from them. Then, when the books had blown up, he'd hired a social media team to keep the cogs of the shit-machine turning. Everything was at one remove from him... even eventually the stories themselves, when he'd hired a couple of ghost writers.

But he'd felt unable to escape from the shadow that Sikene and Nobody had shed over his life. He wrote his own stuff under his own name and got nowhere. And even though only a handful of people on Earth knew that underground horror writer Gavin Swainey was the IP owner of the *Miss Nobody* brand, he still felt as if he would never make his "own" way until...

They were both dead.

A Gordian solution.

Gavin had begun his plan to end the saga of the sexorcist and her Siamese sibling, Sikene.

One last book, set here, in his home town, utilising a creature from local folk lore to ultimately kill off his literary creation.

Tonight it would end.

But as he wandered amongst the immense crowd of readers who so obsessively loved his work that they would travel across continents to be here this night, he wondered...

Was he doing the right thing?

All around him he saw people from so many nationalities, so many different backgrounds of ethnicity, and class, and creed, all focused on one thing that united them and made them one big, happy family even if they could not speak a word of one another's language, because they all shared a world... a world that Gavin had created.

A world he was going to have destroyed at midnight.

*****

Out on Above Bar Street, at the main entrance to West Quay, the protestors had started singing another hymn, watched carefully by a number of rank and file police. Amongst them was Gideon's mother, though she was not joining in with the singing of "Nearer My God to Thee" because she wasn't feeling well.

She couldn't have easily described the sensation. At the start of the evening she had felt elated, uplifted, when she and a dozen members of her church had arrived to swell the ranks of the good Christians already there, those who had turned out to protest against the Satanic foulness of the *Miss Nobody* books and their abhorrent author. All her life she had felt that the world was becoming a dimmer and more Godless place, and yet felt helpless to do anything about it... and now, to find herself amongst other wholesome minded people who had chosen to take a stand, however slight, against the encroaching darkness, she had felt her spirit soar. They were her to do His work in an age where so many had turned their backs on righteousness.

But about an hour or so ago her mood had soured.

No.

That wasn't it.

About an hour ago she had felt... something awful.

A sort of *wrenching*.

As if some vital part of her had been ripped away.

Though she could never have phrased it as such, even within the confines of her own mind, the sensation had its roots in her womb, and was kissing cousin to the nausea of menses and the early weeks of pregnancy.

She had nearly passed out. She had had to sit down on one of the camping chairs her church group had brought for their older members comfort, accepting a flask of lemon tea and a couple of her friend Mrs Suresh's vegetable samosas.

Now she was standing again but she didn't feel like singing, even though this was one of her favourites.

The feeling of (*something awful*) had not gone away. It had been slowly changing, it seemed, as slowly as the hour hand of a clock.

It had mutated into full blown dread.

There was a burst of static from close to the entrance doors, doors which were politely but firmly barred to the protestors by a small cluster of police officer's in their hi-vis yellow jackets. Beyond them, visible through the glass, thronged the perverted fans of *Miss Nobody*, dressed as devils and demons.

The static was from one of the police officer's radios. She answered it, her expression a little bored.

Somebody somewhere began pounding a drum. A big drum, a bass note *boom... boom... boom... boom...*

Gideon's mother felt herself unable to look away, even though she could not hear the radio or the officer over the sound of singing and the drum.

She watched.

The dread ballooned.

The officer's facial expression underwent a number of changes as the unheard conversation between her and the dispatcher took place.

Resignation.

Puzzlement.

Amused contempt.

Light indignation.

Anger.

Again, puzzled, but this time mixed with disbelief.

And then somebody screamed.

Gideon's mother turned, and a razor made of ice drew the length of her spine.

It hadn't been a drum.

As with most humans, her experience of reality was limited, and when confronted with something that destroyed the boundaries of her world, her dull mind attempted to render it in imagery it understood.

Her first thought was "elephant."

Grey. Enormous. Charging. Unstoppable.

Boom... boom... BOOM... BOOM...

Her second thought was "angel."

It was human shaped.

It had wings.

It had an erection of raw, skinless flesh the size of a man jutting from between its thundering legs.

Her third and final thought before dumb animal terror overwhelmed her brain was a sequence from a nature documentary she had seen once.

She loved nature documentaries.

There had been a snake, and there had been an egg. The egg was several times the size of the snake's head. Then the snake's jaw had unhinged, allowing its mouth to open impossibly wide and engulf the egg.

The great grey thing that was filling up the whole world suddenly made sense of how she felt, and just before sanity was lost to her, Gideon's mother knew both that her son was dead and that she'd be joining him imminently.

*****

They were not wings, that which grew forth from his back, though their shape was vaguely similar. The fleshy off-white canopy that stood forth was more like a cancer that patterned its tumour growth on a spider web, glistening with slime.

Ascupart did not know or care. He was only a biological machine collecting genetic material. He had eaten much along the way, but the more he ate the more he wanted to eat. As he grew, and as his flesh distorted –his crotch bulged then burst then grew forth and *hardened*- so did the hunger.

Vast symbols hung across the face of the structure in front of him but he barely registered the twisted shapes that meant WEST QUAY because clustered before it, screaming and screaming, was more food than he had encountered in seven thousand years.

And within the structure a feast beyond imagining.

*****

If PC Moores had been any sort of policeman, humanity might have had a chance.

Astra had explained that the monster had known her name, her real name; it had called her "Star", which only her mum and her piece of shit brother ever did.

Her piece of shit brother was well known to the police of Southampton, a minor thug on the Lords Hill estate by the name of Ray Webster, also known as Cunt Face. Suspected of more than he'd ever been caught for, principally stealing motorcycles and mopeds.

PC Moores did not put this evidence together.

He and the other attending officer's at The Hobbit had watched the CCTV footage recorded in the garden barely an hour before, and each had gone through some of the classical stages of grief.

Denial;

"No way, no, that can't be real, it's some sort of joke or stunt, or..."

Anger;

"Right, enough of this! This is just some sort of bloody prank and I am not putting up with it! You lot are just trying to make us look like mugs, aren't you?"

Bargaining;

"It's just a wind-up, right? Yeah? Just tell us the truth and we'll see that this goes no further, right?"

And finally, acceptance;

"It's real...it's fucking real..."

But by the time this brilliant piece of police work was concluded, the call for all units to make their way to a major incident at West Quay was already being broadcast.

Yes, if PC Moores had been more of a policeman he might have already ascended through the ranks. He also would have put together everything that he now knew and would have realised he was the only one with any clue to what was actually happening.

Or at least, he knew of a lead he could follow. A lead that, if followed, might have given them all a chance of surviving.

But instead, that chance was hanging on the wall of a small study in a flat not too very far away...

Useless.

*****

The entrance to West Quay was a huge concourse lined with shops, an entire high street indoors. Most of it now was thronging with fans in costumes of their favourite characters from Miss Nobody's pornographic adventures.

Midnight was fast approaching.

Not only a new book, but also an appearance by Miss Nobody's reclusive creator!

The excited talk was all around the newest book. Rumours and gossip and alleged online leaks were traded by the eagerly swaiting readership.

At two minutes to midnight, the central entrance was smashed inwards, the automatic doors that had been guarded by police against intrusion by the protestors out on Above Bar street being *kicked* inwards and skidding across the ground in a welter of twisted metal and broken glass.

People screamed and drew back from the carnage.

Even more screamed when they saw what was squeezing its way inside.

Ascupart's winced at the bright lights, momentarily stunning him. Outside, the glow of streetlamps had not bothered him as they were few and far between, but after spending a thousand years buried in complete darkness and emerging at night, the sudden glare blinded him.

Blood drunk and dazzled, he stopped where he was, framed by the destruction of his entrance.

The pause was enough to change the mood of the crowd. The initial shock of his entrance had been born of the 21st century Westerner's fear of terrorism; the destruction had seemed to be the result of a bomb blast. Then, this enormous *monster* had appeared, and the only natural response to it should have been fear...

Except this crowd were here because of a love of books that featured monsters.

Monsters being fucked to extinction.

Someone said, "Oh wow, that's so fucking *cool!*" and started taking footage with their smart phone... and the teetering mood of the masses instantly switched to cries of delight and shocked laughter and a hundred more devices being pointed at the gore-drenched giant that stood blinking in front of them.

The buzz was instant and all encompassing.

Of course, a grand spectacle, the last *Miss Nobody* book being released with a hell of a bang, some kind of animatronic puppet, special effects, hey this must be the monster she's going to sexorcise, it looks so real...

A few fans had even done there research into local Southampton folklore in anticipation of guessing the plot of the final book, and could name him.

The giant, Ascupart.

They took selfies, made lives streams, and updated their social media accounts whilst he tried to gather his wits.

All over the world, pictures of the thing became freely available.

An elephant, a foetus, an angel from Hell.

It looked vastly pregnant... which made no sense, because it also had an erection.

Upon this, impaled from arsehole to appetite, were three humans bodies, each missing their heads from where Ascupart's titanic cock had torn them off on its way through.

It looked like he had attempted to fuck a human centipede.

So. Fucking. COOL.

*****

Ascupart snarled in pain at the lancing light.

It was almost as intense in his eyes as the sensation of the *glowing* from the little ones in his mind.

Slowly, he became accustomed to the brightness.

His mind touched the assembled thoughts of the food.

And he was puzzled.

There was no terror of him.

There was only... joy?

This was a new thing. Never in his existence had his appearance inspired anything but terror or hatred.

His confusion held him in place a few minutes more, enough time that the food was suddenly swarming eagerly around him.

Words, impressions;

YAAAASSS GOT TO GET A SELFIE

OMG CHECK THIS OUT FOLLOWERS R U JELLY?

HASHTAG MISS NOBODY LAUNCH HASHTAG MONSTEROTICA HASHTAG HELLO BIG BOY HASHTAG...

Nonsense, a tsunami of chattering gibberish.

What had become of this species?

It didn't matter. He sensed he was almost done.

He grinned.

The genetic material went crazy, redoubling their efforts to capture every moment of this amazing spectacle.

Ascupart picked one up.

All he felt from it was intense excitement, laughter, happiness... it was waving as he lifted it, mugging for the envious fans below who wished they had been included in the performance but who never once stopped pointing their smart phones at him.

The fan's name was Simon McHardy. He'd flown all the way from Tasmania to be here because the *Miss Nobody* books had been his favourite source of wanking material since he was a teenager. Being picked up by the giant puppet, to be included as an active part of this amazing show, was the best thing that had ever happened to him.

Wait 'til I tell all the cunts at the pub back home!

Ascupart gripped him with both hands, one around his chest and the other around his legs, twisted him twice like administering an Indian burn and pulled him apart.

The lipless mouth sucked the contents out of the upper portion like slurping the bean sprouts from inside a spring roll.

The giant felt a change in the collective consciousness of the genetic material. The glows around him grew brighter, sharper.

A sudden wave of uncertainty.

He brought a foot up and stamped on one. It thought of itself as *GERHARD JASON GEICK*. Blood squirted between the giant's toes and star-burst across the floor around his sole.

He stomped another, a *SEAN HAWKER*. The Hawkman's final thought was of *Alice's Adventure in Wonderland*, when the girl shrunk after drinking from the bottle labelled 'Drink me'; *"Why, I must be shutting up like a telescope!"* He felt his head crushed down into his throat, his throat crushed down into his chest, his chest into his belly and his legs snapping under him and then darkness as his brain was finally crushed.

Ascupart wrapped a fist around the root of his cock and drew his hand upwards, pulling the corpses off like stripping the meat off a kebab skewer.

The general mood was tilting from uncertainty to something else.

With the dead stripped off, he quickly grabbed a gaping food nearby, inverted her, and shoved her face first onto his cock like she was a condom instead of a living, breathing, thinking creature.

Her name was Marian Elaine, a psych nurse from the US who was also one of TikTok's most beloved book reviewers.

Marian's head was crushed up into her chest by his glans, and then Ascupart pulled her inside out sheathing himself.

The crowd finally panicked.

Adrenaline flavoured the material.

Ascupart patted his bloated belly with one hand, causing the contents that were still alive to scream, and with the other he masturbated with the inside out corpse. Then he began to waddle after the fleeing sources of DNA.

The crowd could not move fast, the press of bodies impeding any escape.

Many stumbled or fell behind.

Christina Pfeiffer had made the pilgrimage all the way from Alaska to be present at the launching of the final *Miss Nobody* book. She'd come dressed as a slutty wendigo.

Ascupart grabbed her.

Wrapped in his huge hand, Christina had just drawn enough breath to scream when the giant placed the tip of his thumb under her chin and popped her head off her shoulders like flicking a grape into the air.

Flicking a grape up to catch...

The brain survives quite a while after decapitation. Christina's world tumbled over and over as her spun on its ascent, then arced down again as gravity took hold.

She was even able to think, *Well this sucks,* before she tumbled into the monster's upturned and open mouth.

He caught her on his huge tongue.

She blinked.

She'd landed on her cheek, looking back up and out of the mouth over twin rows of teeth.

This really sucks.

Ascupart lifted Christina's headless body over his gaping jaws and squeezed her belly.

Her lungs and heart and liver and stomach and the ropey length of her intestines sprayed out of the rugged stump of her neck into the giant's mouth and buried the fan's still thinking and feeling head in a pile of her own hot viscera.

The crowd was still screaming and trying to get away. Many had fallen and been trampled, unable to get up as Ascupart hefted his growing bulk.

He could barely walk.

He threw himself forward onto his bloated gut, crushing the limbless and maimed protestors who hadn't already died inside him. One of those, Gideon's mother, might have recalled another one of her beloved nature documentaries if she'd seen what Ascupart did; in Antarctica when a giant leopard seal would throw itself forward onto an ice shelf after the tiny fleeing forms of the penguins it was hunting.

Fallen fans saw him coming and cried out for help or mercy as the giant's mouth gaped wide and began to gnash.

He swung his arms out on either side of a dozen struggling bodies, men and women, and swept them all like winnings at a card table towards himself... towards his mouth.

The effect was similar to a combine harvester.

Ascupart champed and chomped and chewed as fast as his jaws would let him, cramming the screaming fans into his face in a tangle of clutching limbs and pleading faces which shredded between his teeth in a sea-spray of blood and bone fragments.

Amongst those being eaten alive was Gavin Swainey himself.

The texture of his thoughts was lost amongst those of his readership who were dying along with him, but there was a certain amount of self-reflection underneath the animalistic horror.

The final book in the long-running *Miss Nobody, Sexorcist* series did in fact feature the eponymous heroine coming to Southampton to fuck the resurrected giant of local legend, Ascupart. Unfortunately, Miss Nobody finally met her match, and the giant fucked her to death.

And now, the writer was about to be snuffed out by that very same figure from folklore!

Ridiculous, thought Gavin as teeth snapped through his shin bones.

Preposterous, even, he decided as the teeth sheared through his pelvis and genitals.

If I were to write of such an over-the-top coincidence, I'd be crucified in reviews, he reflected, as the teeth crunched through his ribcage.

Any further thoughts were truncated by the next bite that burst his head.

Both hands pressed the last few screaming people into his vast mouth, and Ascupart lay on his expanding stomach for a few seconds, chewing and swallowing the thrashing morsels.

More.

More.

MORE.

Yes... more.

He was not quite full.

MORE.

*****

PC Moores had managed to palm the fat goth slag off onto useless old Des Lynch, but Jack was refusing to leave his side, even as the call for all available units to report to an incident at West Quay came in.

The units that had been stationed at the shopping centre for the big Sikene book launch had gone silent.

"Jack, son, I'm on the clock, you can't come with me..."

"I'm coming," said Jack.

"Look, stay here with what's-her-face... Star, stay here with Star and Officer Lynch, Des, you remember Des right?"

He was eager to be away, to get to the scene of the action, to be in the midst of whatever was really going on. Ambition still rode high in his heart, still believing that tonight was his chance.

Monster's weren't real.

Fucking fairytales.

"I'm coming," said Jack.

He didn't need his weird son around being weird.

"*You aren't!* Look, whatever's happening here is, is, this is an active investigation..."

"I saw inside its head."

PC Moores blinked.

Behind his eyelids he saw the CCTV footage from the garden. The great grey thing squatting amidst the carnage.

Monster's aren't fucking real!

"It's called Ascupart," said Jack.

His father stared at him.

"You what?" he asked quietly.

His son was making eye contact with him. Jack never did that. It was part of his autism. But now he was staring hard at his father, and there was a kind of flat, awful understanding behind them.

"Its mind touched mine. I saw what it is."

PC Moores rubbed one hand down his face.

"Jack, don't be stupid mate, I..."

Jack suddenly leaned in close to his father and spoke softly.

"I'm coming with you."

The police officer felt a shudder pass through him; there was something dangerous in his son's voice, an inflection he had only heard from a few people before, most of them nasty fucking pieces of work.

Jack never showed proper emotions. Most of the time it was like talking to a robot.

PC Moores made a rash decision.

"Fine. But you stay in the car."

*****

A couple of lines had become half the baggie and before she knew it Alana Laurie was completely off her fucking tits.

This wasn't the first time she'd passed out after snorting a little too much ketamine.

When she came too she was shaking and sweaty and had no clue where she was.

Too bright. Wincing.

Her back and her neck ached.

She blinked against the light, letting her massively dilated pupils get back to normal so she could actually see.

At first she did not recognise her surroundings. And then she remembered everything.

She was sat on a toilet in the staff breakroom of the Waterstones book shop in West Quay where she was supposed to be giving her final appearance as the reclusive authoress Pinky Sikene.

She groaned.

Oh Jesus, how long was I out? Shit! Did I miss the signing? Shit, I won't get paid! Shit!

She sat up straight, feeling awful, coming down.

She groaned again.

No, wait... I'm the star of the show, right? And the store manager with a face like a slapped arse is in charge. Looks like she plays rugby... probably a lezza. Right. She wouldn't have just let me stay passed out in her for the duration... I must have only nodded for a few seconds, five minutes at most.

Alana got herself upright and staggered in front of the sink with a mirror above it.

She looked like she felt.

Shit.

She spent a few minutes reapplying make up and straightening her hair and clothes, then took a deep breath.

Her nerves were gone, at least. A ketamine low knocked all over problems towards the back of the line.

She still had the rest of the baggie.

Fuck it. If this was her last turn as Pinky Sikene, she wanted to sparkle.

She railed the rest.

The next time she looked in the mirror, she saw a young woman who had the world by the balls.

Confident, she left the toilet.

The staff break room was empty. No sign of the lezza store manager.

Weird.

What was her name?

Fizzing with ket, Alana made her way down a service corridor towards the staff entrance to Waterstones, encountering no-one.

Stranger still, she heard nothing. Earlier, the excited hum of hundreds of people had been coming through the walls. It had acted as a brown-note that had triggered her nervous guts in the first place.

But now... nothing.

Okay, this is fucked.

She gingerly pushed the door open and peeked out.

The book shop was empty of people.

The place was also in disarray; many displays had been knocked down, sending avalanches of books across the floor.

They looked like they had been walked over.

Cardboard cut-outs of Miss Nobody, "standees" as they were known, advertising the midnight book release, were knocked to the ground.

These too looked trampled by a great many feet.

Alana stepped into the bookshop.

She almost called out, and then some ancient instinct held her tongue. But it was not strong enough to override her curiosity.

She made her way through the shop.

She stepped out into the concourse that lead either right, towards one of the shopping centre's back entrances and a Costa Coffee on the way out, or left, back towards the smain hub of shops and escalators and the food court on the third floor.

If you walked left, back into the heart of West Quay, the tiled floor rose ever so gently; the giant building sloped down towards the docks.

A red snake was coming down the slope.

No.

Not a snake, though it moved slow and sinuous.

Red.

Exactly equidistant between the shops on one side and the shops on the other –Menkind, The Regenerative Clinic, Timpson, Flannels, Zara- a trickle of blood was slowly slithering its way towards Alana, pulled by gravity.

She watched it pass within a few feet of her, slowly meandering, it's flow guided by the smooth gutters between the floor tiles, like it was an exhausted shopper heading for the exit after a heavy few hours of buying shit it didn't need with money it didn't have... the capitalist dream.

She watched it snaking to Costa Coffee, and then turned her head to follow its trail back up towards the main hub of the shopping centre.

A faint scent came from that direction.

Alana's parents lived in a small traditional village, a place that was almost a caricature of the notion of an English idyll It had a post office, a pub, and a small parade of shops between the two.

One of those was a family owned butchers.

Scent is the sense most closely linked to memory, and for just a moment Alana was there, outside Baynham's & Son's with its displays of chops and joints and sausages in the window.

And then she was back in the present, in an eerily quiet shopping centre just after midnight that had previously been absolutely choked with people.

Now there were no people, but blood, and the smell of opened flesh.

Against sanity and logic, she began to walk towards it. Even with evidence of an atrocity, curiosity compelled her.

It was unreal, therefore she had to see.

She walked parallel to the track that the blood trickle had made, passing by clothing shops on either side that who windows were filled with headless mannequins dressed in this season's soon to be discarded trends

As the floor levelled out slightly and the concourse widened, ready to become the great central hub and heart of West Quay with escalators and elevators allowing access to all four levels, she saw the source of the blood trickle.

A blood lake.

It lapped around the legs of tables and chairs outside a YoGoo! frozen yoghurt place that was the last shop before entering the central hub. Ahead, Alana could see kiosks selling sunglasses and mobile phone cases, and her view was further obscured by support columns for the escalators

Alana had been shopping in West Quay earlier in the day, doing some light retail therapy before psyching herself up to become reclusive millionaire smut writer Pinky Sikene. The central hub was a wide sort of courtyard space, open all the way to a glass skylight fifty feet wide four levels above. She pictured that central area as it had been hours earlier thronging with people heading for the elevators or the escalators to continue their shopping on other levels, stopping to consult free-standing maps that showed which level and in what direction every shop was. The clamour of conversations, laughter, muted arguments, people eating, had seemed to fill the whole place right up to that ceiling so high above, the air divided by multiple escalators criss-crossing from one level to the next whilst the glass boxes of the elevators serenely carrying human cargo up and down.

Now the only sound was her shoes clicking on the tiles.

No.

Not quite.

There was something else... a low note, very deep, rhythmic and yet raspy too. Laboured breathing, if the lungs were the size of body bags.

Something huge struggling to breathe.

The scent was so much stronger now.

A butcher shop doing a roaring trade.

If she wanted to see where the blood was coming

(*no I don't want to see please I don't need*)

from, she would have to step into it, and walk just a few feet around one of the huge support pillars to see what could be seen.

At this point, Alana knew she was still passed out in the Waterstone's staff toilet. She was passed out and having a nightmare, because only in nightmare's do our bodies betray our minds and freight us towards the horror.

The blood seemed to kiss the soles of her shoes as she stepped into it, walked through it, an inch deep. Wet kisses, *smack, smack, smack.*

It was a malformed hot air balloon, deflated on one side and nearly bursting on the other. The side that was swollen was stretched so tightly that the contents could be seen through the thin skein of grey skin.

There was some kind of huge white net or ragged ship sails extending behind the mammoth bulk, splayed across the blood drenched ground and lying over smashed kiosks.

Alana's mind tried to make sense of what she was seeing. It made comparisons, but nothing made total sense of what the thing was.

A crashed hot-air balloon, yes, for its size and general shape. But also a lava lamp for the way the contents roiled and twisted.

Contents that had once been people.

A few were even still alive, though the eyes staring out of dissolving faces pressed against the translucent skin had mercifully surrendered sanity.

If the thing *had* been a hot air balloon that had crashed down through the skylight high above what would have been the basket on one side opened red eyes and stared at her. A split tongue slowly slithered across bared teeth.

Fee fi fo fum...

Alana pissed herself, though she was not in immediate danger, for Ascupart could not move.

Finally, he was full.

His body began the metamorphosis.

The thing that Alana had thought was a great white nets or ragged ship sails began to twitch, to rise.

Twitch, rise... and curl.

The growths that had resembled rotting wings or cancerous spiderwebs slowly began to wrap around his vastly bloated body.

It's a boy.

A strange thing for her mind to note, but yes. Alana had spotted a skinless erection bigger than her jutting out from under the belly-sac stuffed with churned up corpses.

What had drawn her eye to this organ was that it was starting to ejaculate.

Except...

What was erupting from it with wet, farting sounds were shiny pieces of metal and plastic. Rod shapes, pin shapes, things with bolts through them, oddly jointed pieces, small bundles of wires, all squirted from the enormous cock and fell upon the bloody ground. They were coated in slime to ease their transition.

A foot appeared, sticking out suddenly from the tip of the glans which was bigger than her head. Then, under pressure, the rest of the plastic leg eased out and clattered to the ground.

Surgical implants... Dad fell and broke his leg in three places remember when he was cleaning the gutters and they had to put a bar in to hold the bone together they screwed the broken bits of bone to it and now he walks with a cane and sets off the scanners in the airport that's what you're seeing people's artificial bits being rejected.

...

...

It can't digest them.

An artificial hip and half a dozen silicone breasts implants farted from the cock.

Alana laughed.

"Ha."

Then again

"Ha."

The web-wings slowly sheathed the great bulk of the nightmare.

*****

Jack Moores took the opportunity afforded by that evening's madness to murder his father.

"So what is this thing then?" demanded PC Moores of his son, as he drove too fast, too recklessly. "Ascupart was a giant from a fairy tale, right? A giant like fee-fi-fo-fucking-fum?"

Jack frowned. He'd gleaned a lot during the brief time his consciousness had brushed up against the harbinger's mind.

How to explain?

He was not good at expressing himself.

"It's here to ingest genetic material," he told his father. "It has no choice. That's what it was made to do. Much like I have no choice but to swallow the genetic material you force into my mouth. We are similar in that way... but we are also different, because Ascupart likes it, and I *FUCKING HATE IT HATE IT HATE YOOOOUUU!*"

Somebody who was not Jack could perhaps have made a better job instead of speaking to his father, possibly triggering in PC Moores's mind an epiphany that would have lead the policeman to turn the vehicle around and head back to the place and person who could have helped stop Ascupart.

Instead, screaming those final words, Jack unbuckled his seat belt, lunged, and bit out his father's throat.

PC Moores had heard a wet crunching sound and suddenly knew agony. He'd jerked the steering wheel in shock, mounted the pavement, and slammed into a lamppost doing close to sixty miles an hour.

Jack went through the windshield and had his back broken against the lamp post, spine-snapped and spun around it, his body flung around like a rag doll to come to a rest in the gutter outside a pub.

PC Moores had sat in the driver's seat, his mind trying to process the past few seconds of pain and noise and shock.

Breathing was strange.

He reached up and with trembling fingers found a hole where there had been no hole before.

He felt the blood trickling down his throat. He started to cough as it ran into his lungs, and then he panicked, struggling for breath, beginning to drown in his own blood.

Jack, paralysed, could not move except to lick his lips.

Odd to have his father's blood on his lips, rather than his spunk.

Genetic material.

Fee fi...

Darkness took him.

*****

The official story was, like all the best stories, elegant in its simplicity.

A bomb.

Southampton was a key target for the Nazi war machine during WWII. It had almost been blasted flat during the last years of that conflict, thousands of pounds of ordinance rained down upon it by German bombers making the short and easy trip across the English channel. It was not unheard for bombs to have punched deep into the ground and yet not go off, only to be discovered years and years later during routine maintenance of the roads or during development of brown field sites.

An undiscovered device had been dormant under Above Bar for decades, and that night simple misfortune had caused the decaying explosives to finally awaken. The ancient bomb had triggered an even larger secondary explosion of major gas lines, which utterly obliterated the greater part of the West Quay shopping centre and rendered the rest of the structure impossibly dangerous.

This was the official story, designed to buy time, to keep people out, to keep people from seeing. A story with a beginning, a middle, and a tragic end.

Logical, neat, terrible.

The story held for forty days and forty nights.

Then the chrysalis hatched, and like all newborns, what emerged was *hungry*.

THE END